This Is the Key to the Kingdom

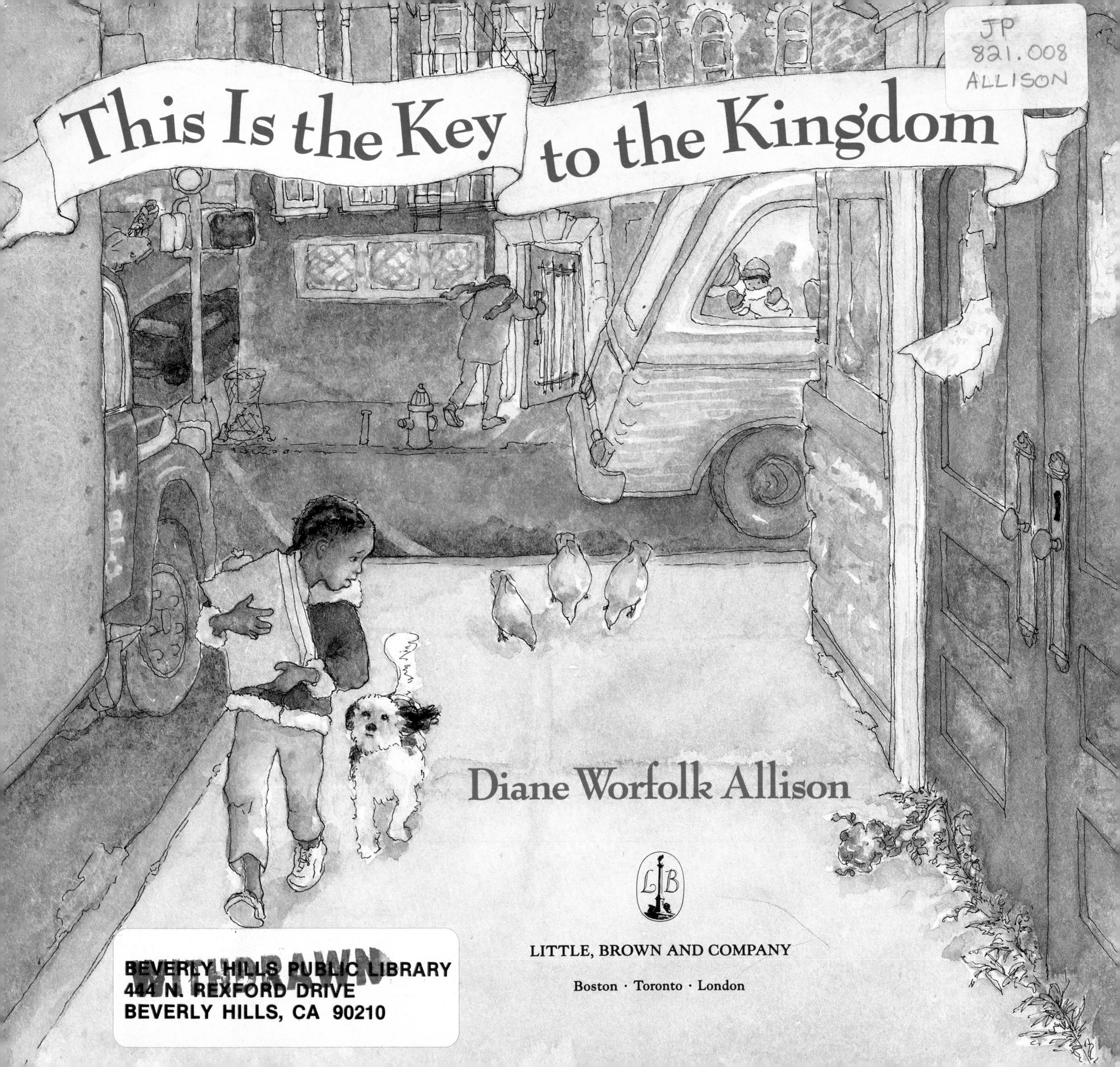

Diane Worfolk Allison

LITTLE, BROWN AND COMPANY
Boston · Toronto · London

For my children, Jessica and Paul,
and those who I remember as children
at the Ezzard Charles School in Chicago;
for Madge and Cam and Ed,
who showed me where the key was when I had lost it;
and for all the children who gave me
their ideas about the kingdom. I used every one.
It may be beyond a hill or behind a door, but every one is here.

WRITTEN AND ILLUSTRATED BY
DIANE WORFOLK ALLISON

In Window Eight, the Moon Is Late

ILLUSTRATED BY
DIANE WORFOLK ALLISON

Chester and Uncle Willoughby

First Edition

Library of Congress Cataloging-in-Publication Data
Allison, Diane Worfolk.
This is the key to the kingdom / Diane Worfolk Allison. — 1st ed.
p.   cm.
Summary: In the illustrations accompanying this traditional
nursery rhyme, a child finds a key and goes on a magical trip
into a landscape filled with color, excitement, and love.
ISBN 0-316-03432-0
1. Nursery rhymes.   2. Children's poetry.   [1. Nursery rhymes.
2. Fantasy.]   I. Title.
PZ8.3.A44Th   1990
398.8 — dc20   89-31573

10 9 8 7 6 5 4 3 2 1

WOR

Published simultaneously in Canada by Little, Brown & Company (Canada) Limited

Printed in the U.S.A.

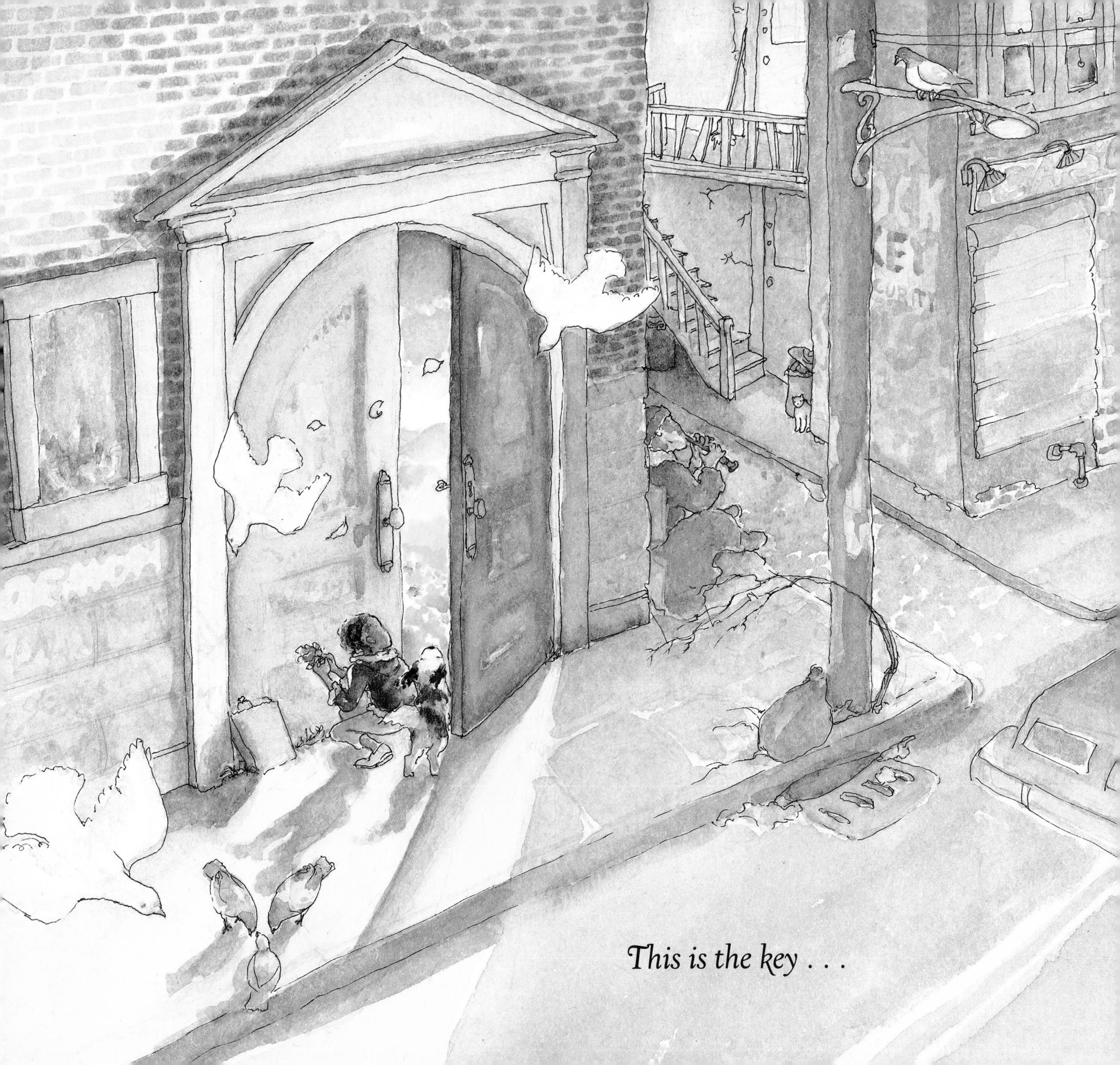

This is the key . . .

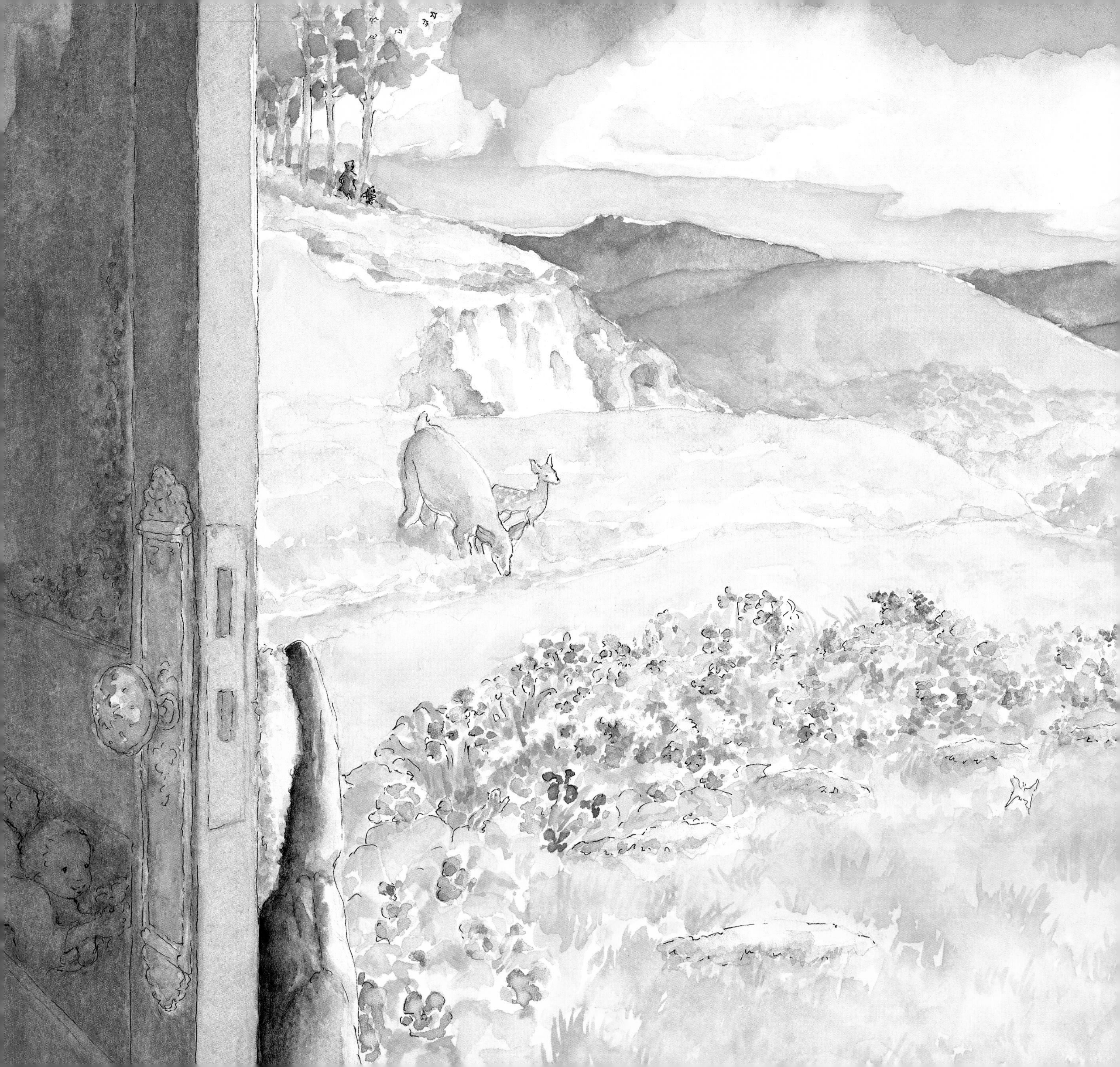

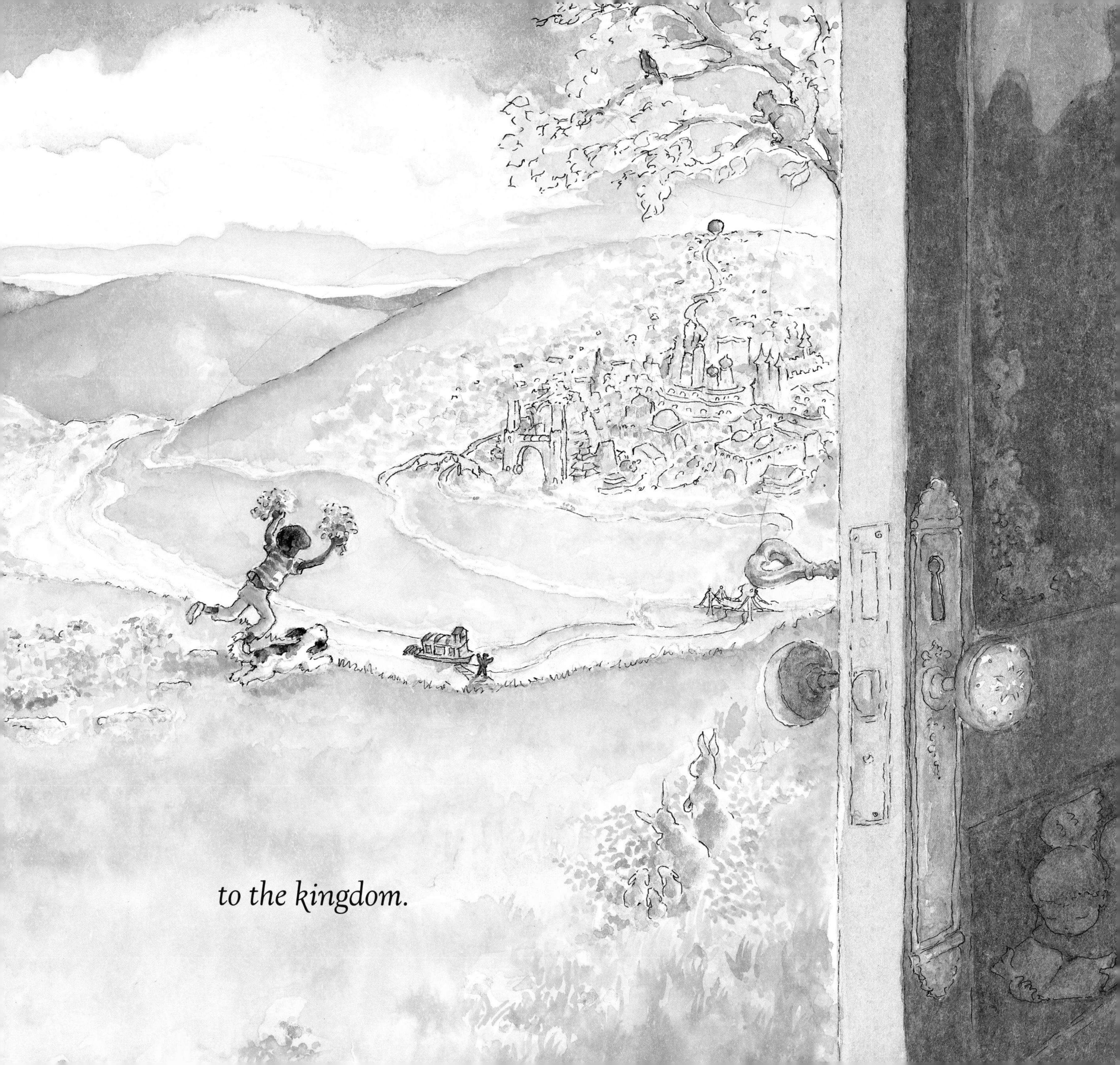

to the kingdom.

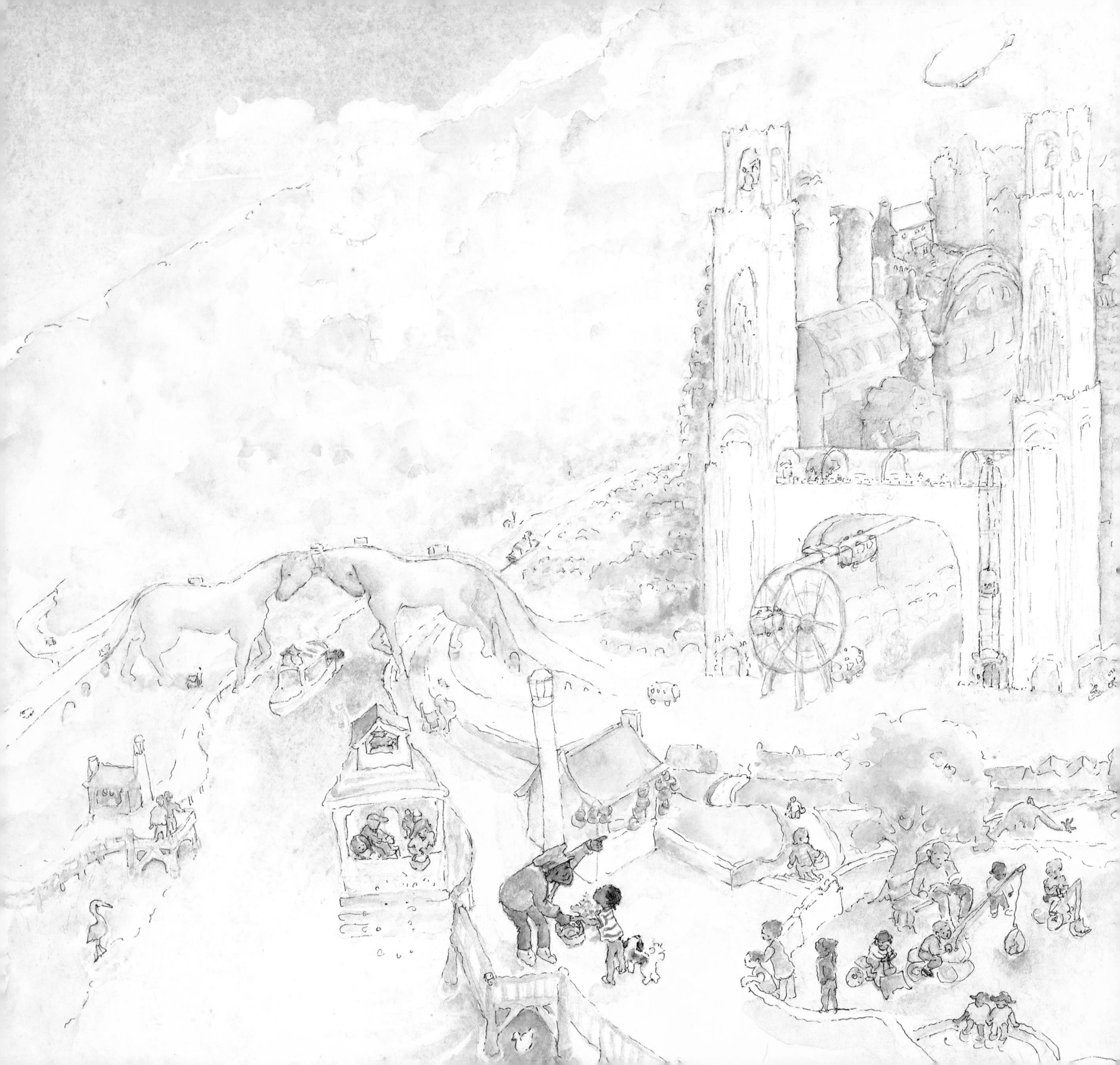

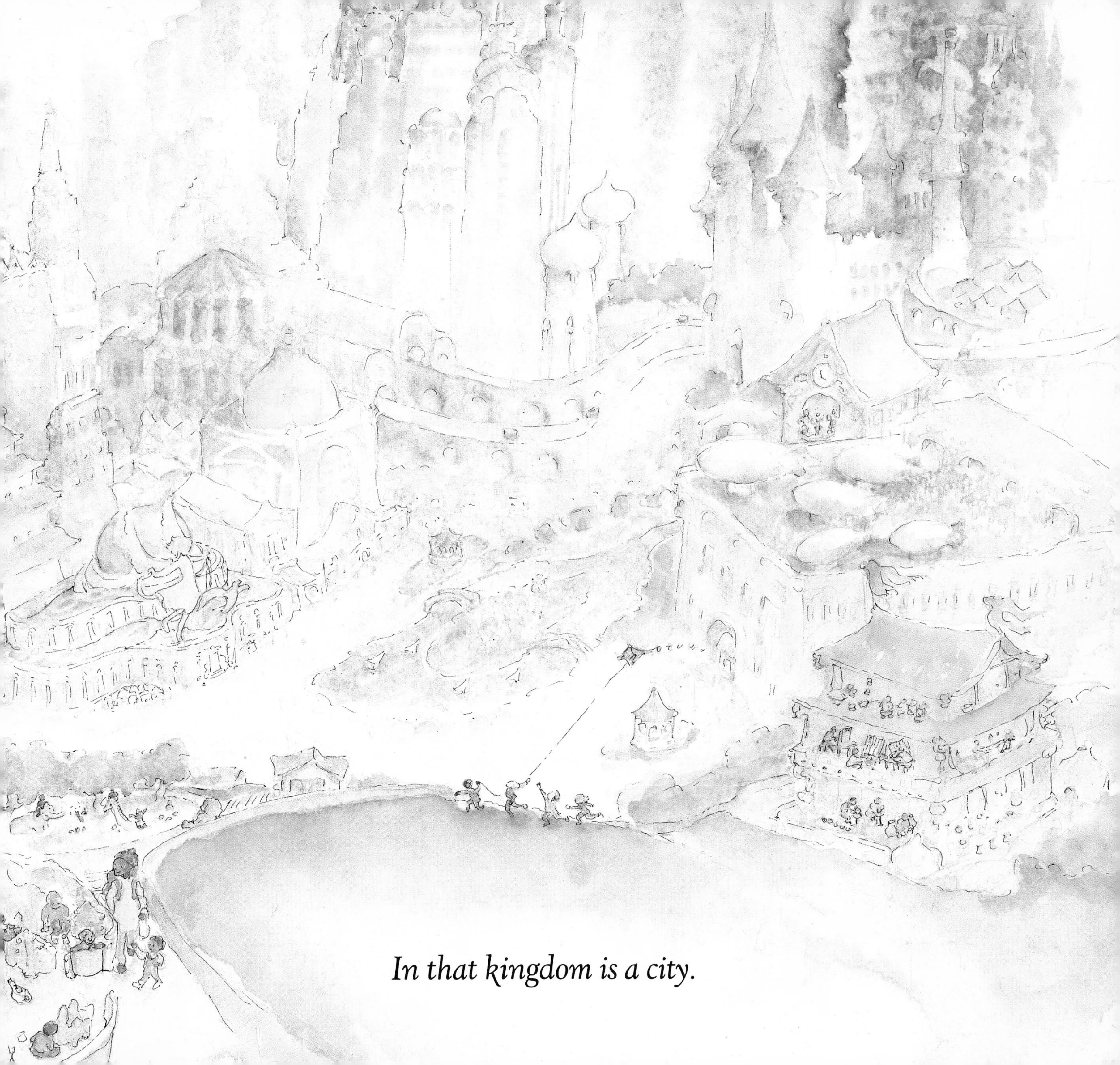

In that kingdom is a city.

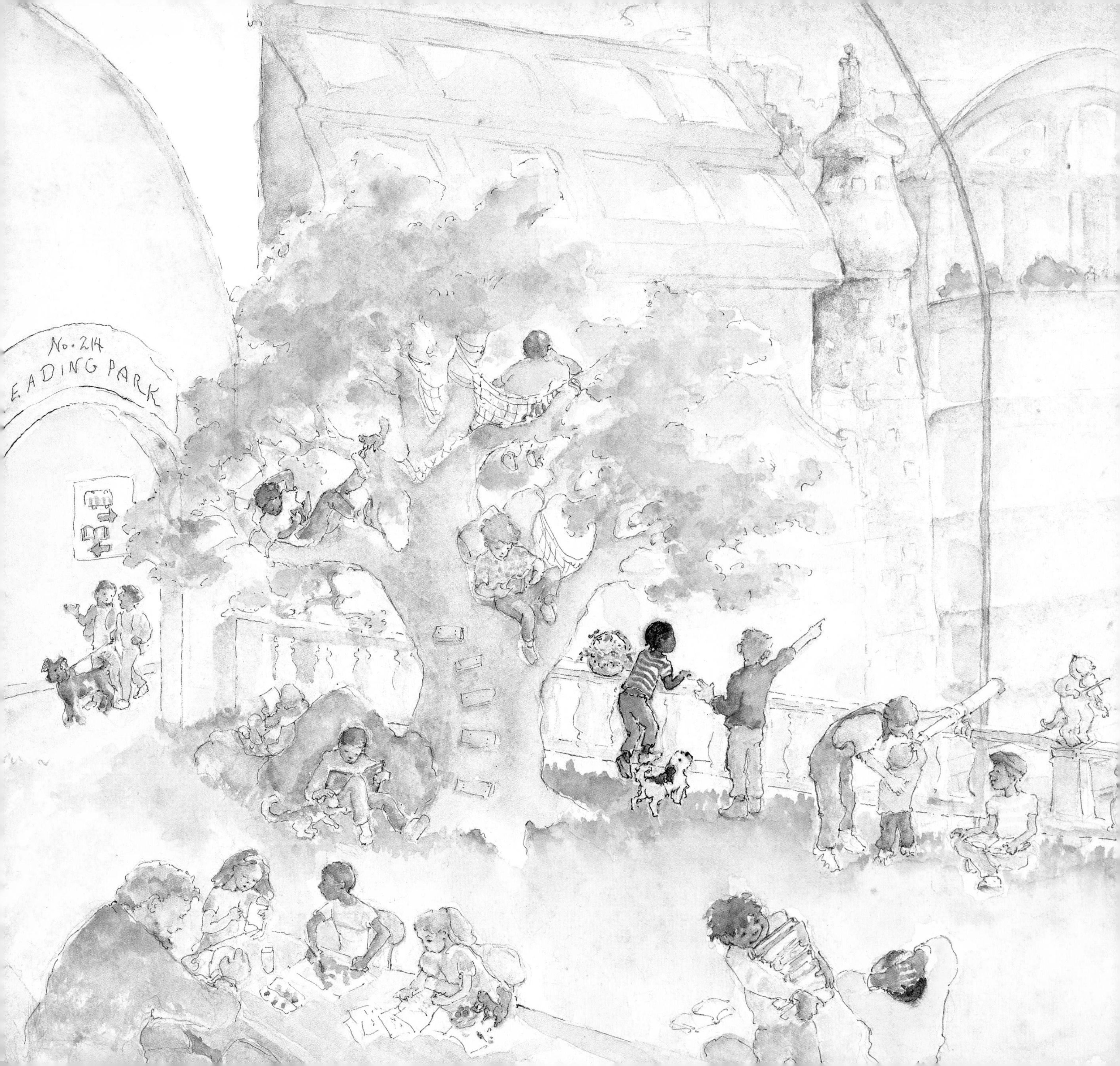
No. 214
EADING PARK

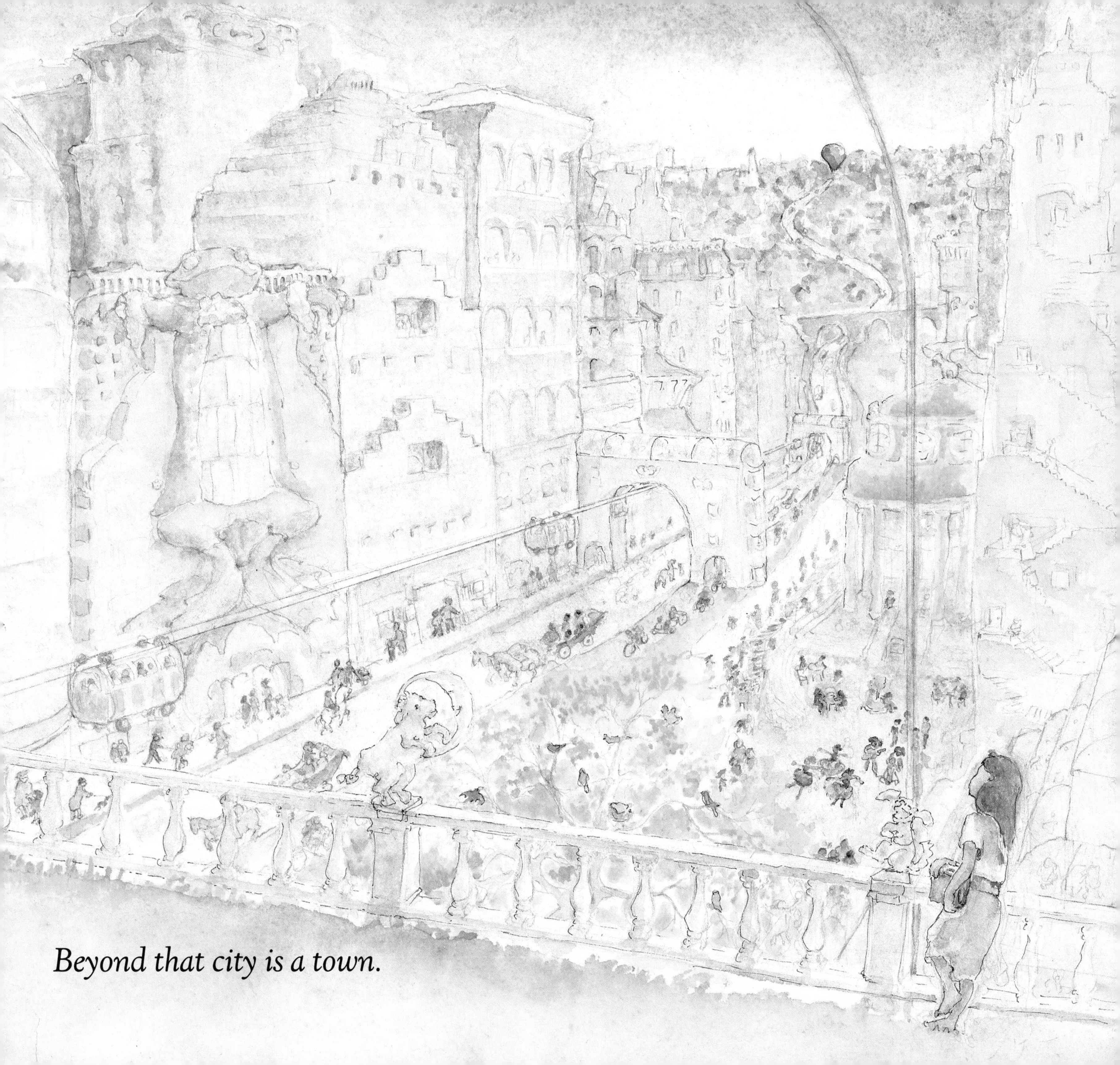

Beyond that city is a town.

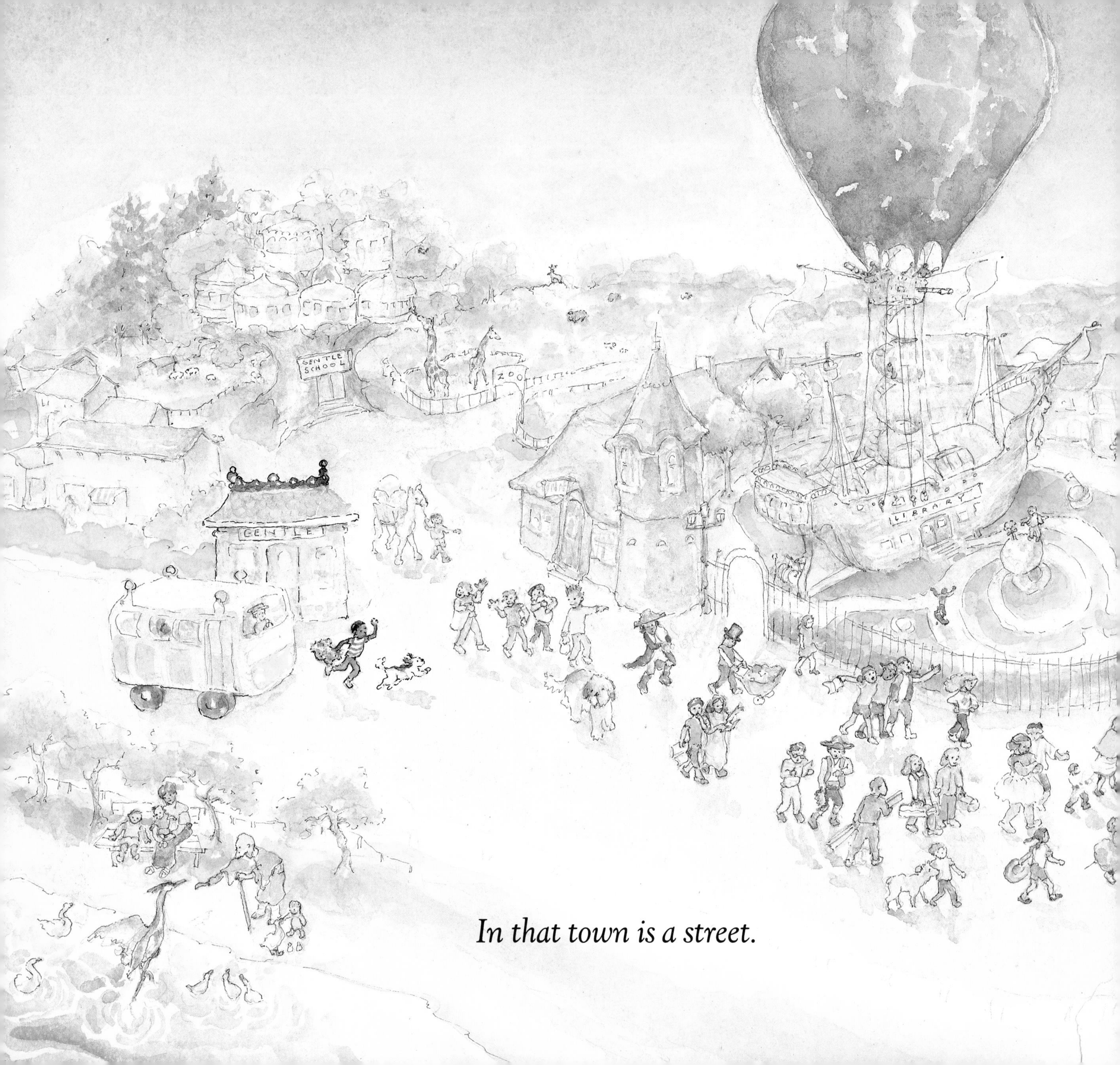
GENTLE SCHOOL
ZOO
GENTLE
LIBRARY

In that town is a street.

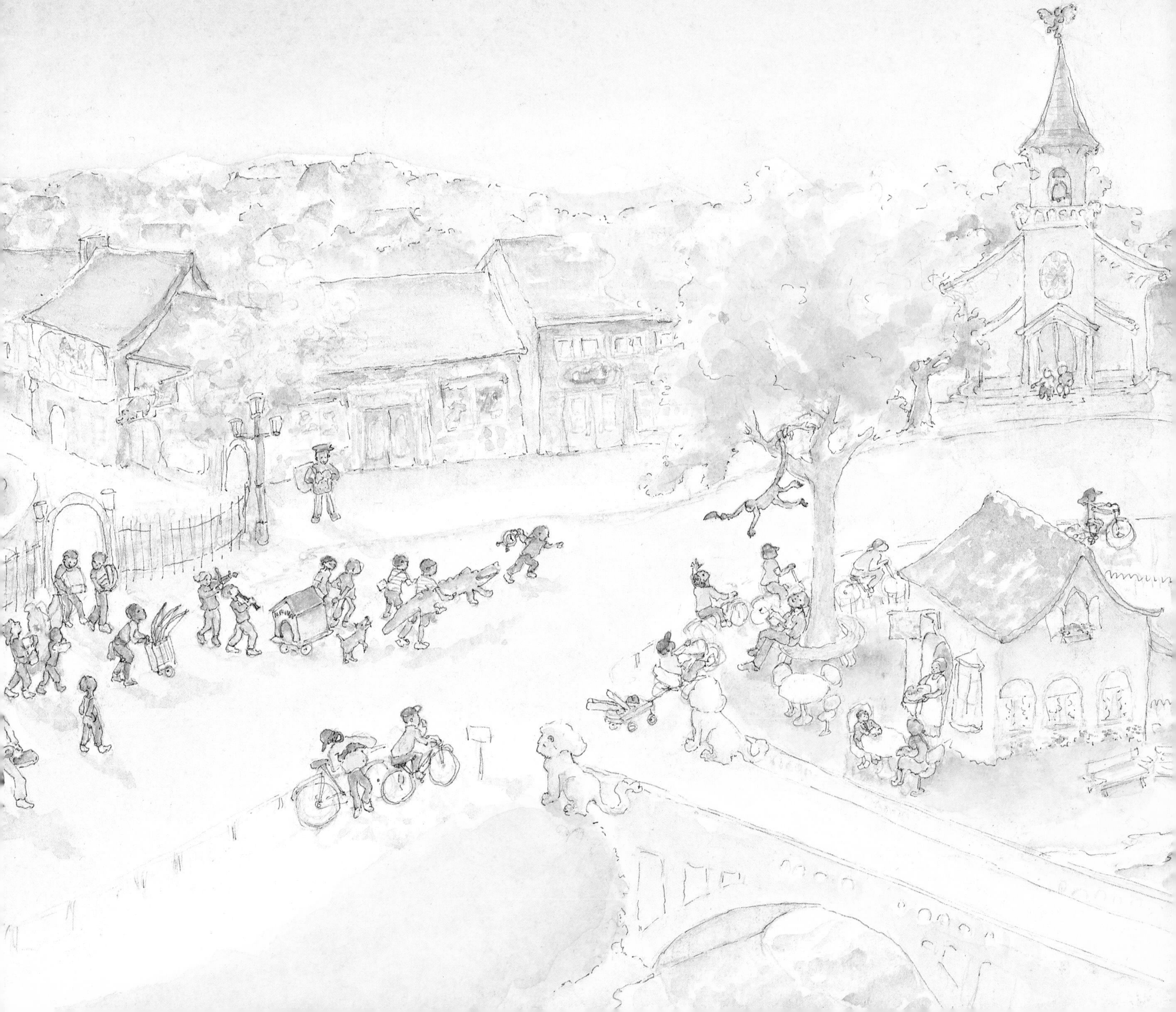

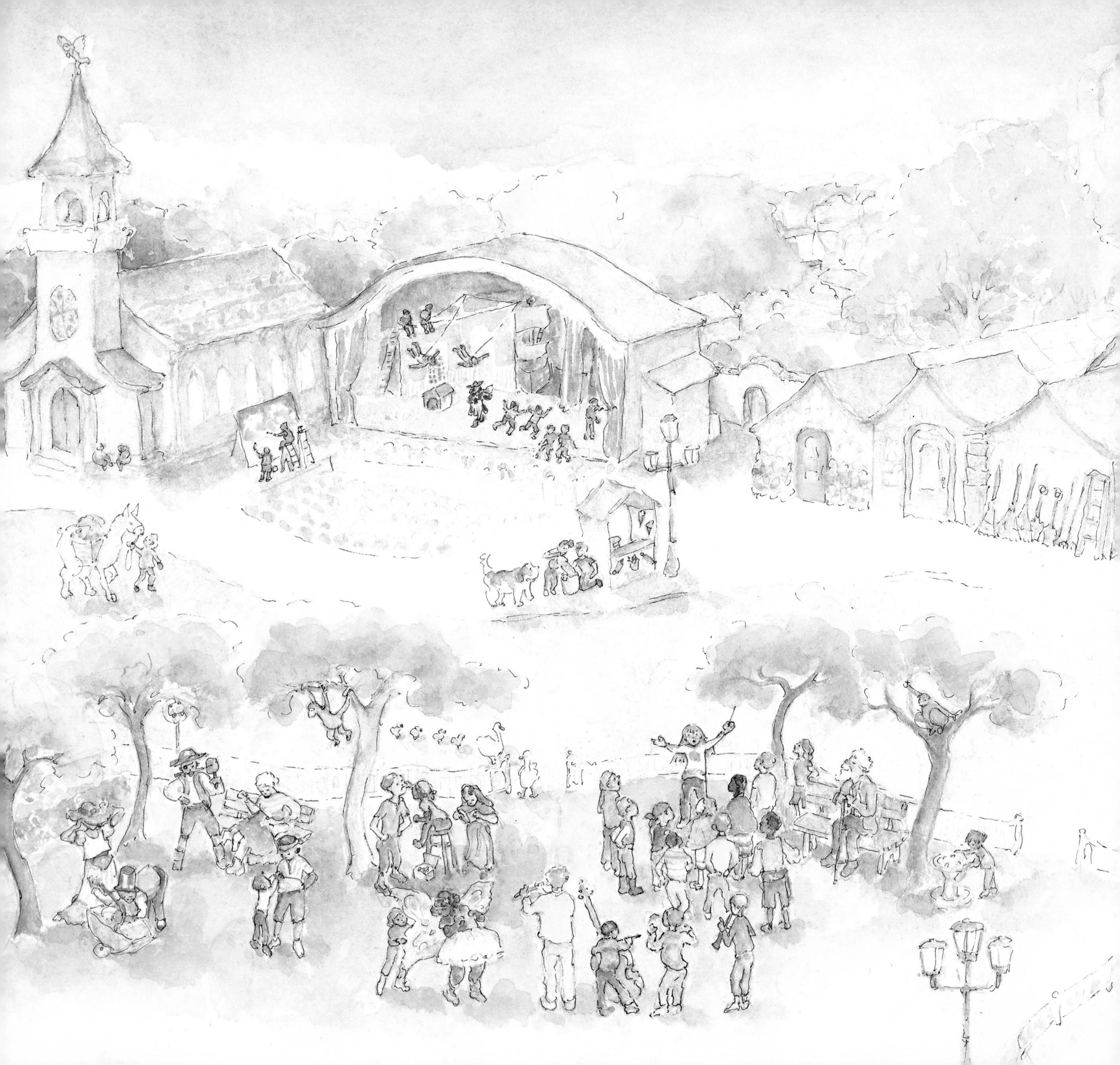

Off that street winds a lane.

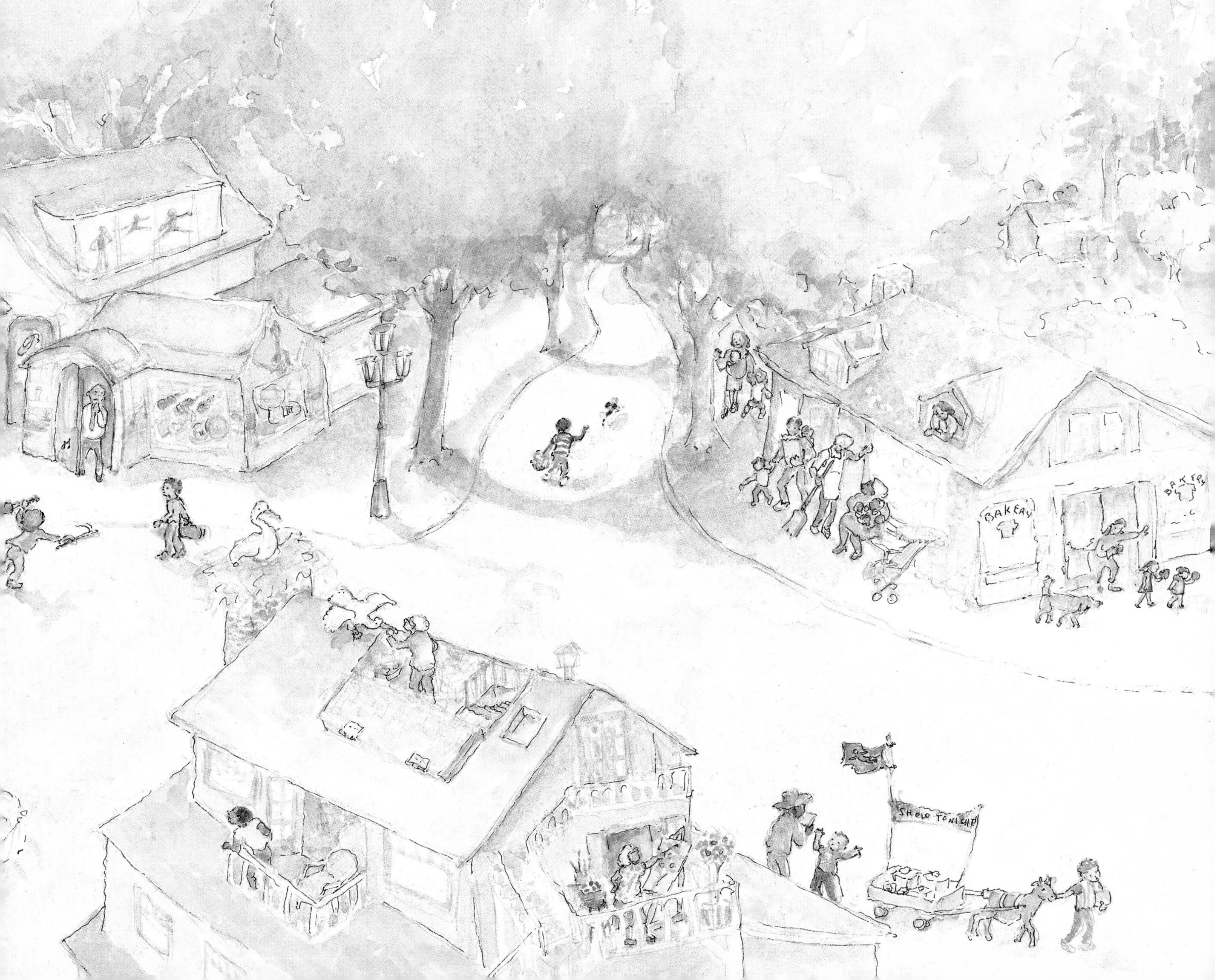
BAKERY
BAKERY
SHOW TONIGHT

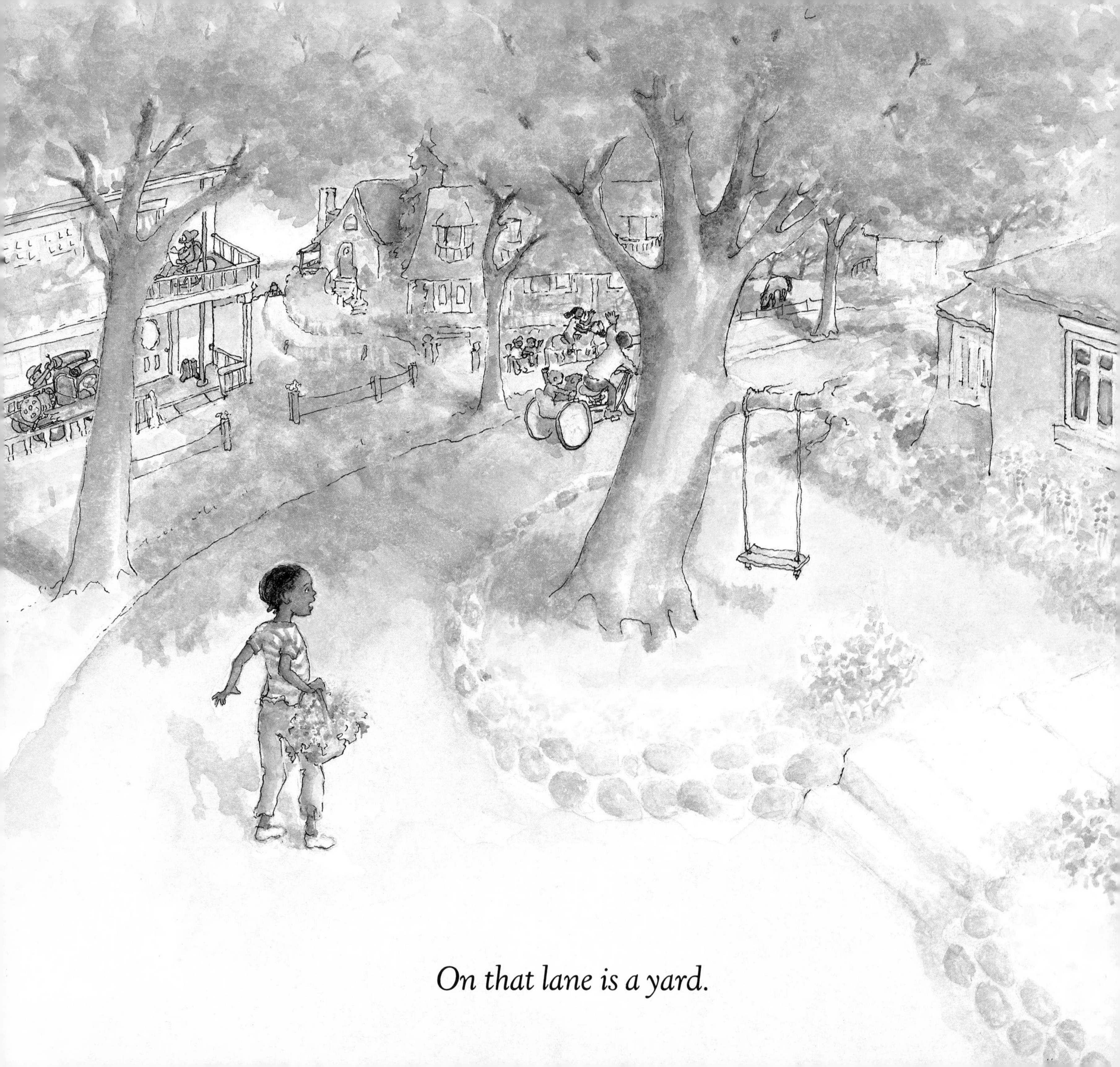

On that lane is a yard.

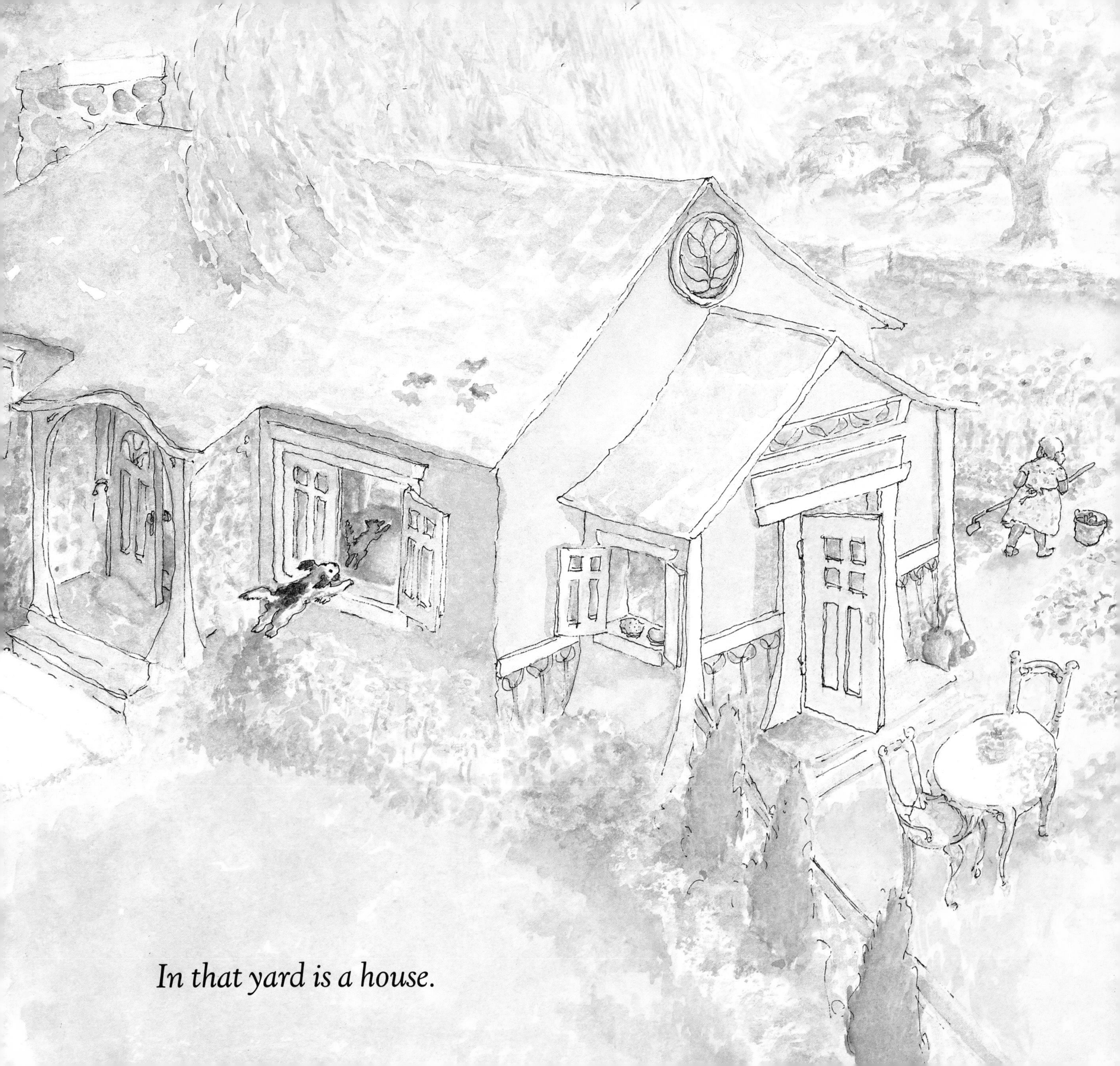

In that yard is a house.

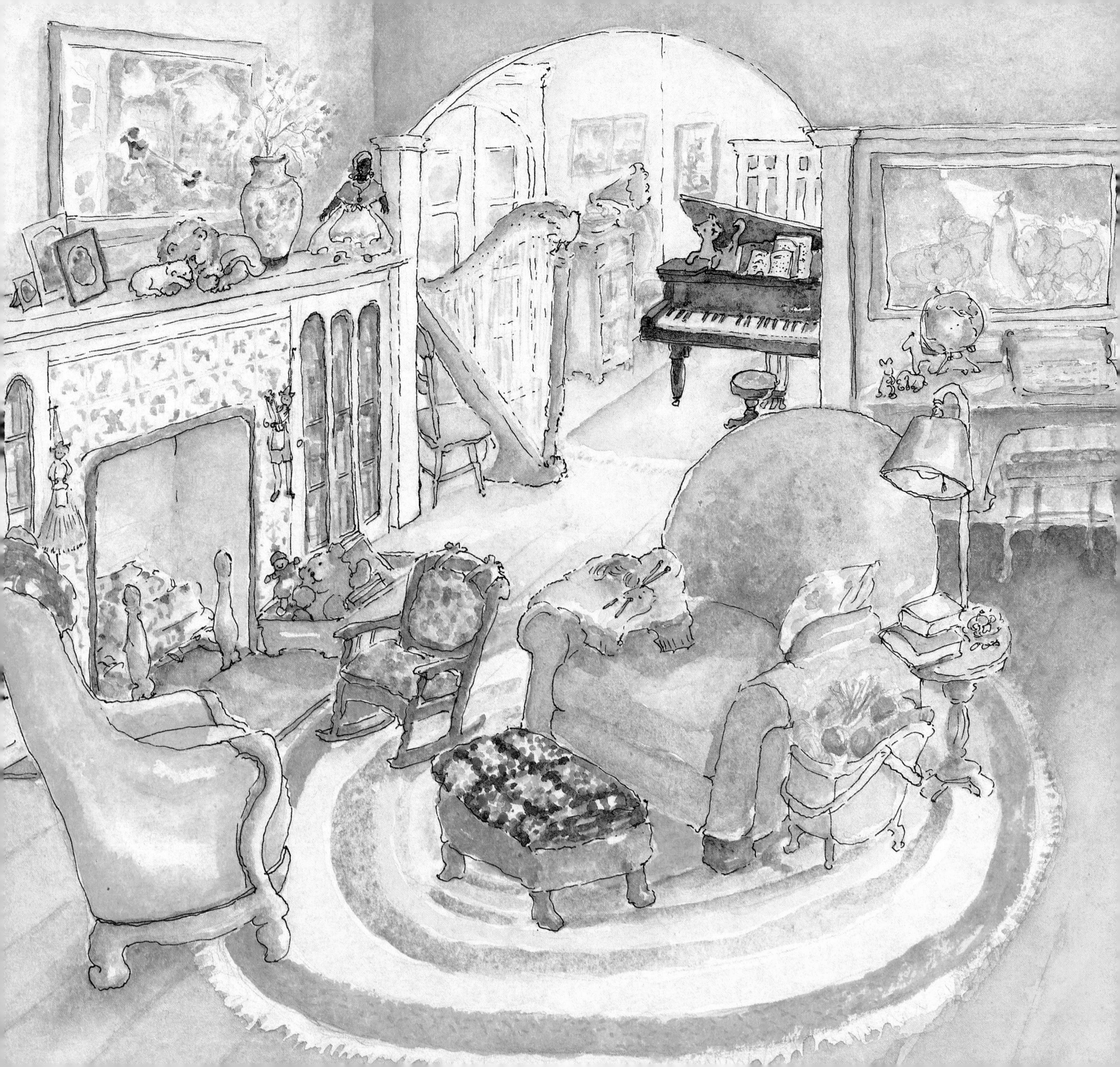

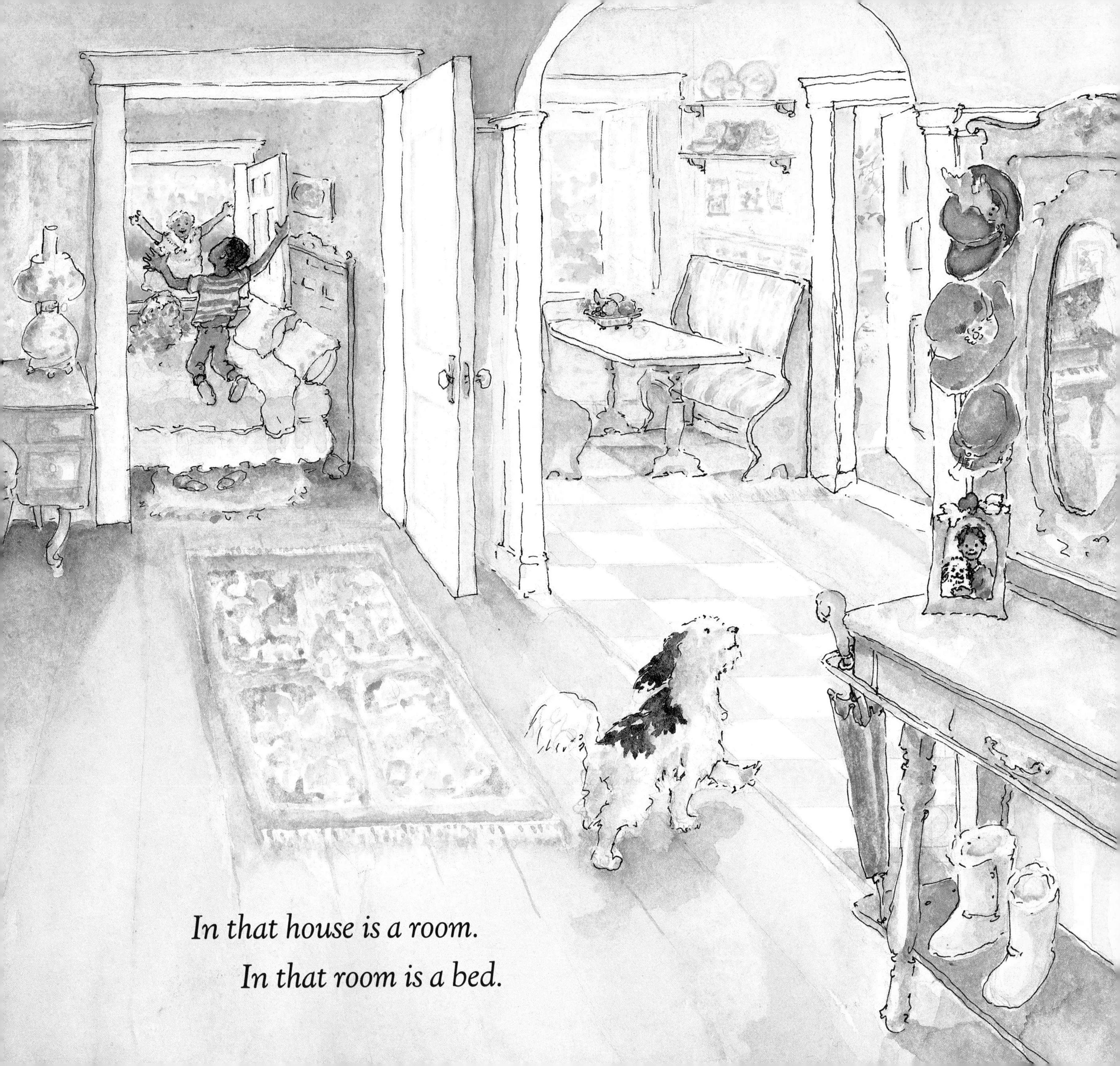

In that house is a room.

In that room is a bed.

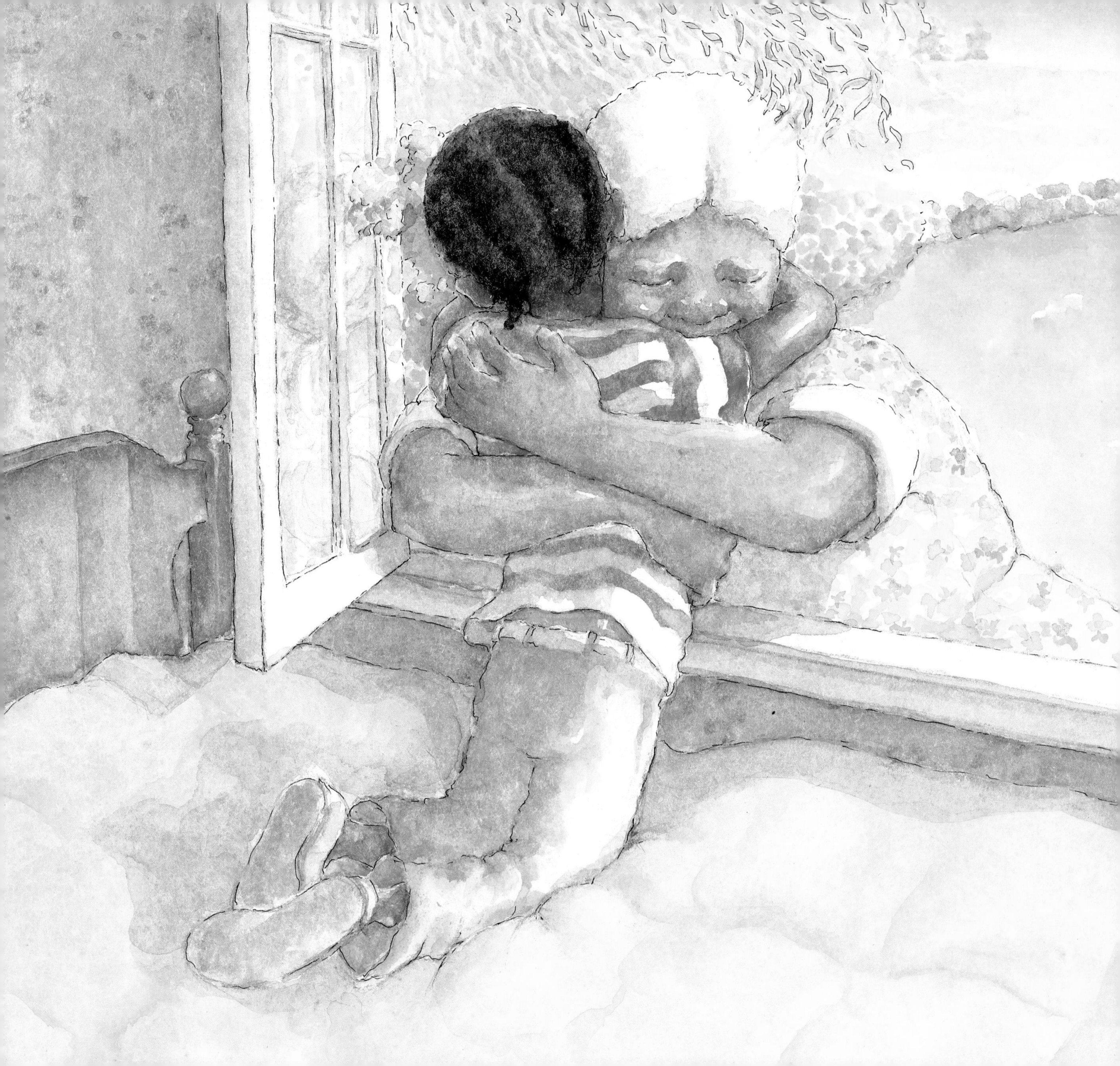

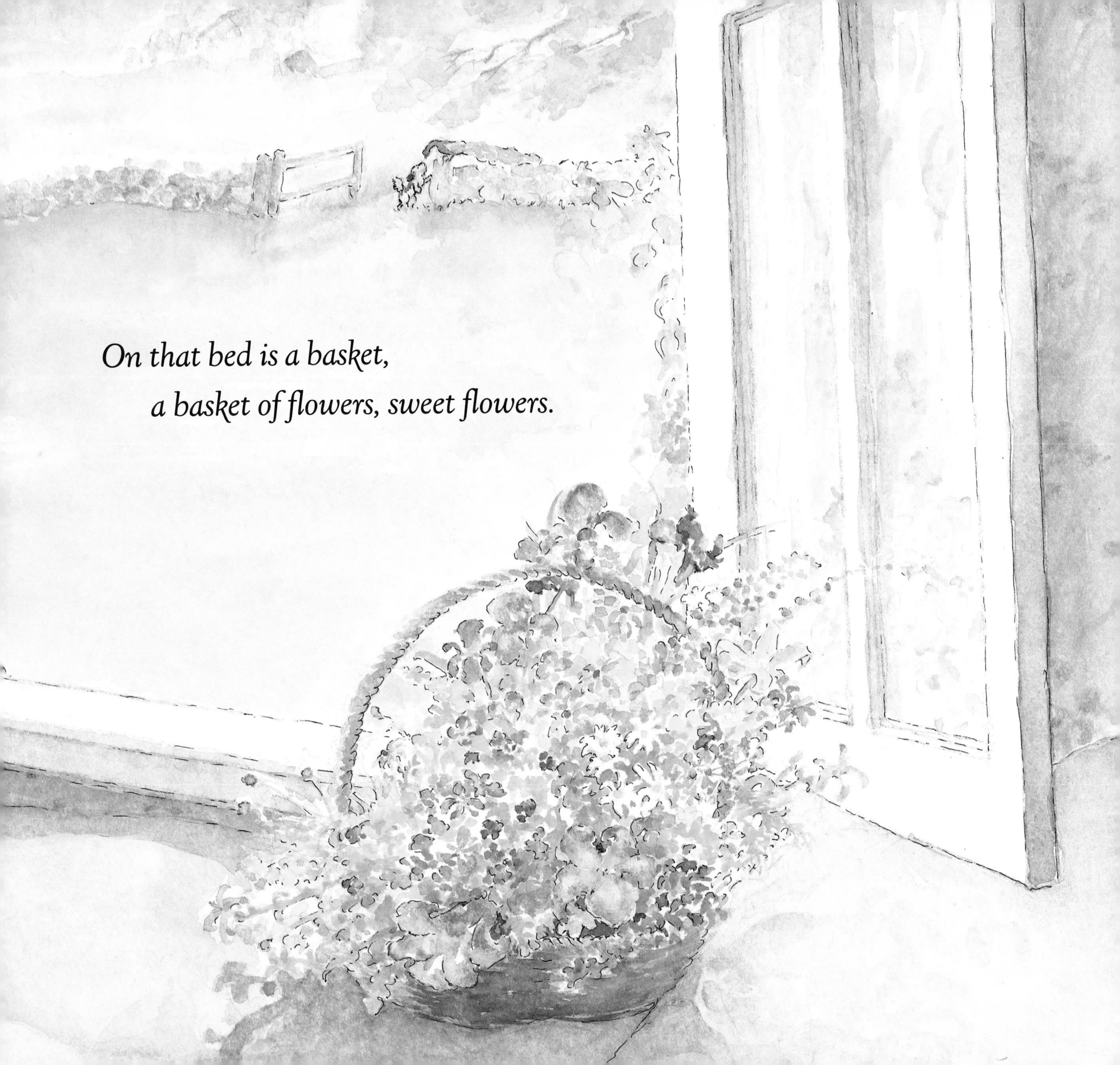

On that bed is a basket,
a basket of flowers, sweet flowers.

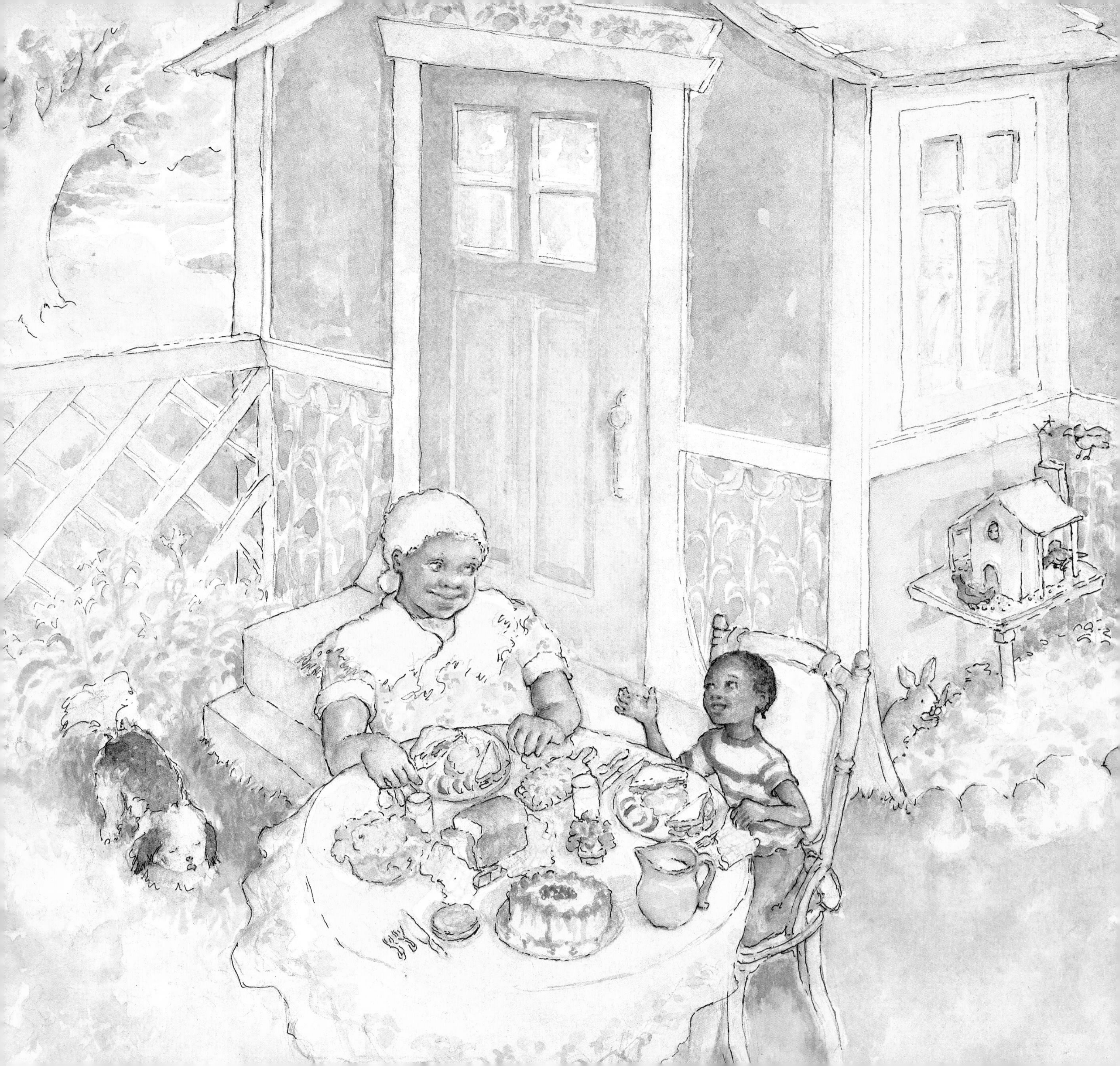

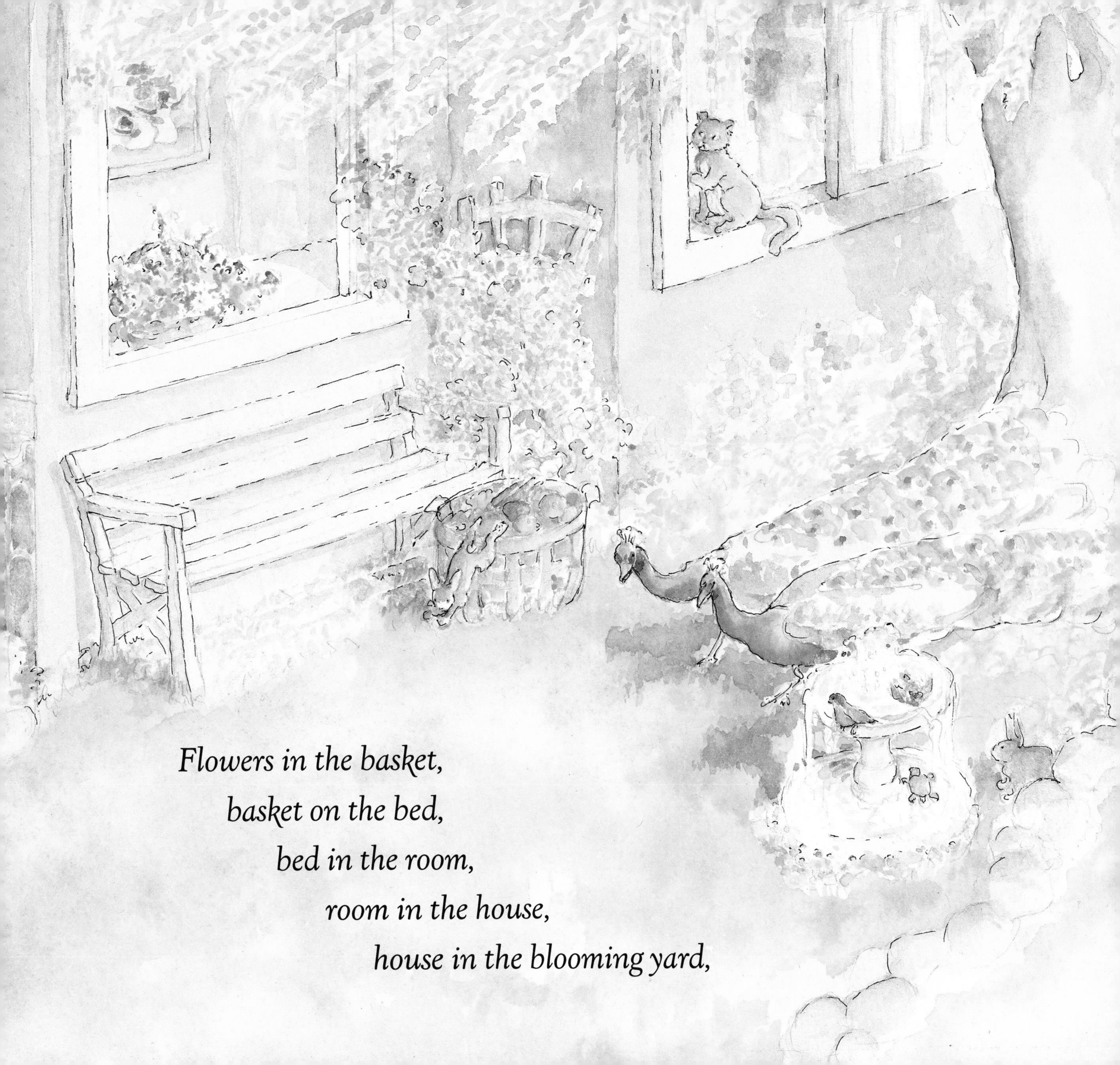

Flowers in the basket,
basket on the bed,
bed in the room,
room in the house,
house in the blooming yard,

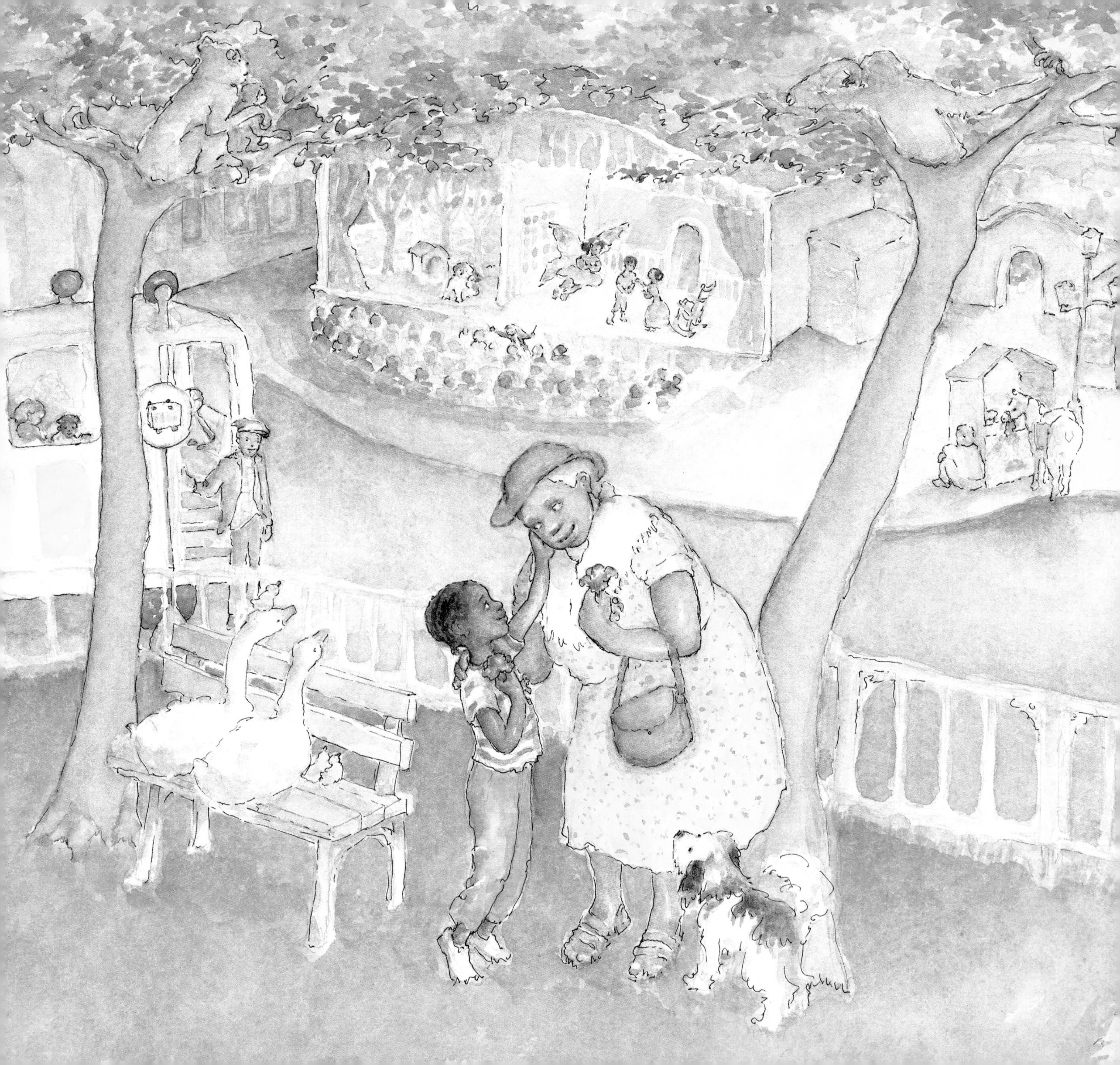

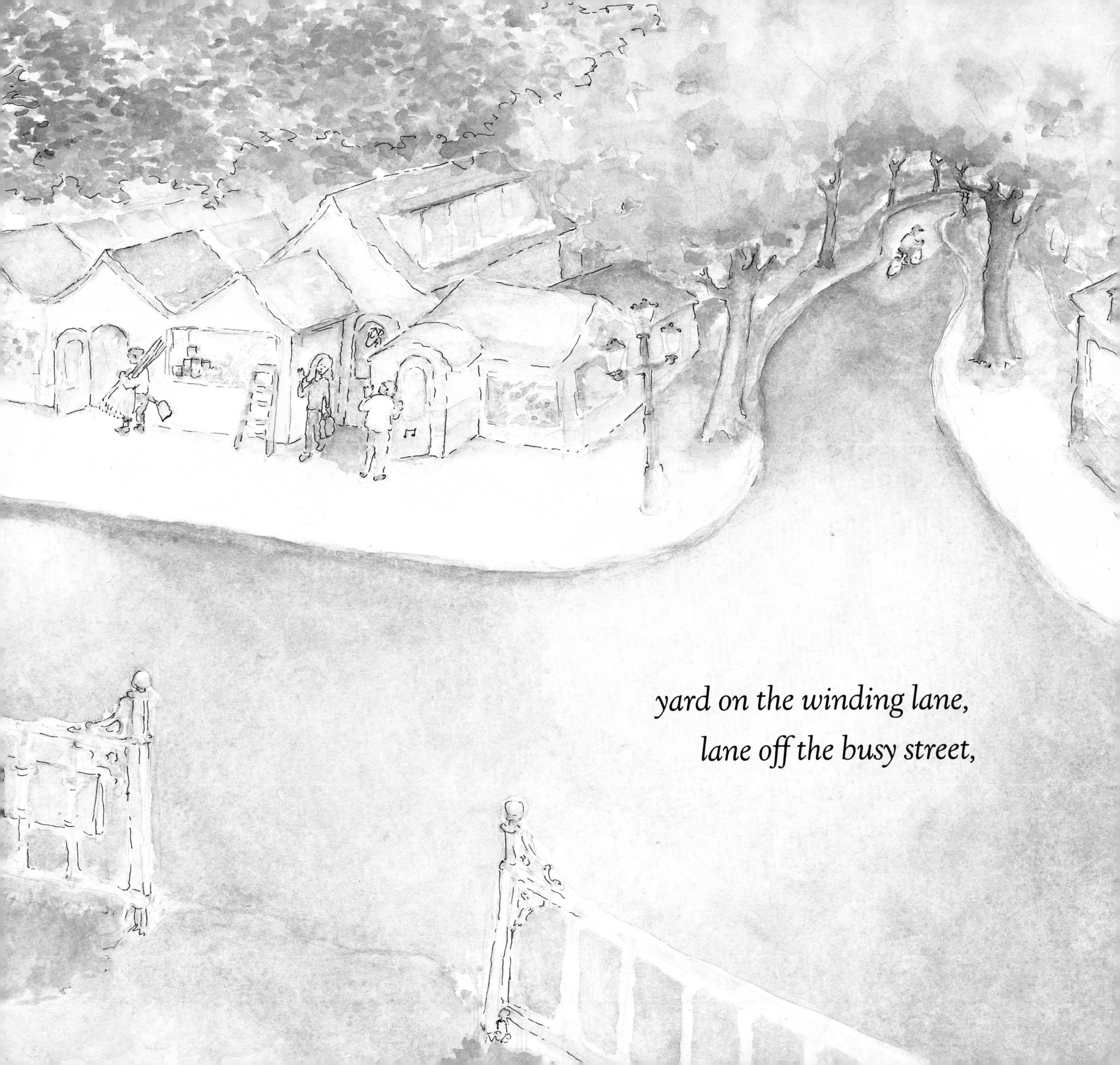

yard on the winding lane,

lane off the busy street,

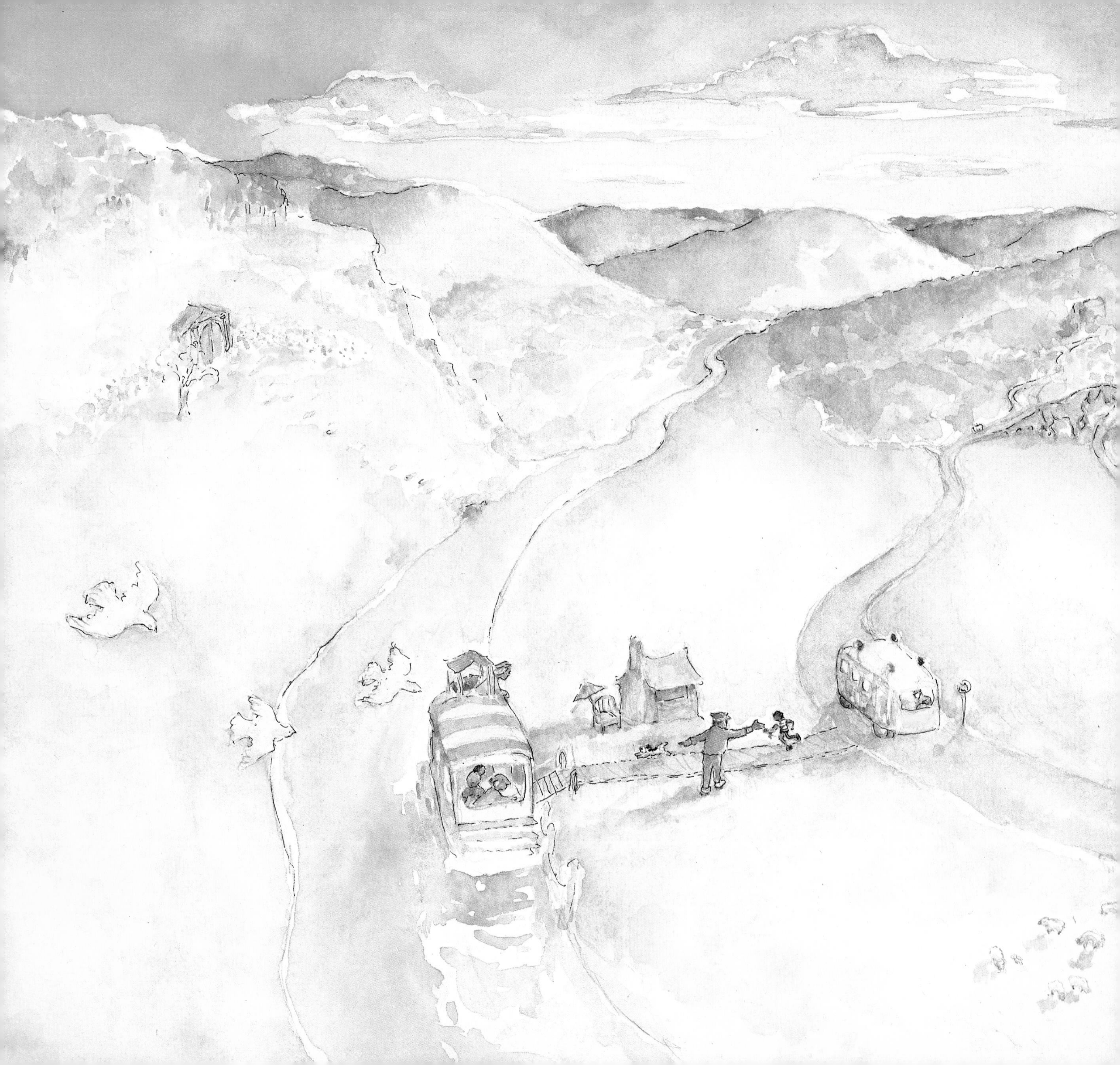

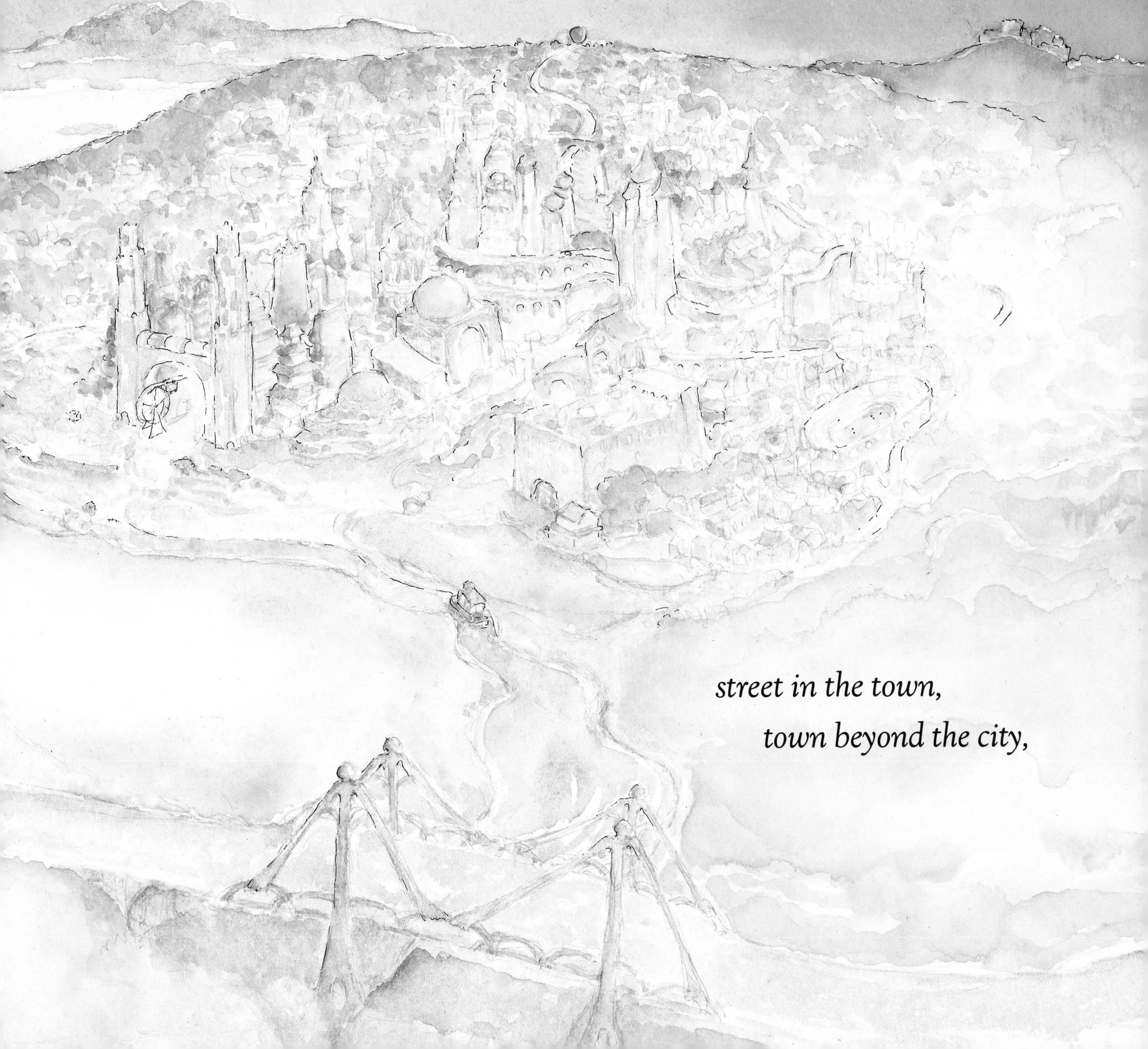

street in the town,

town beyond the city,

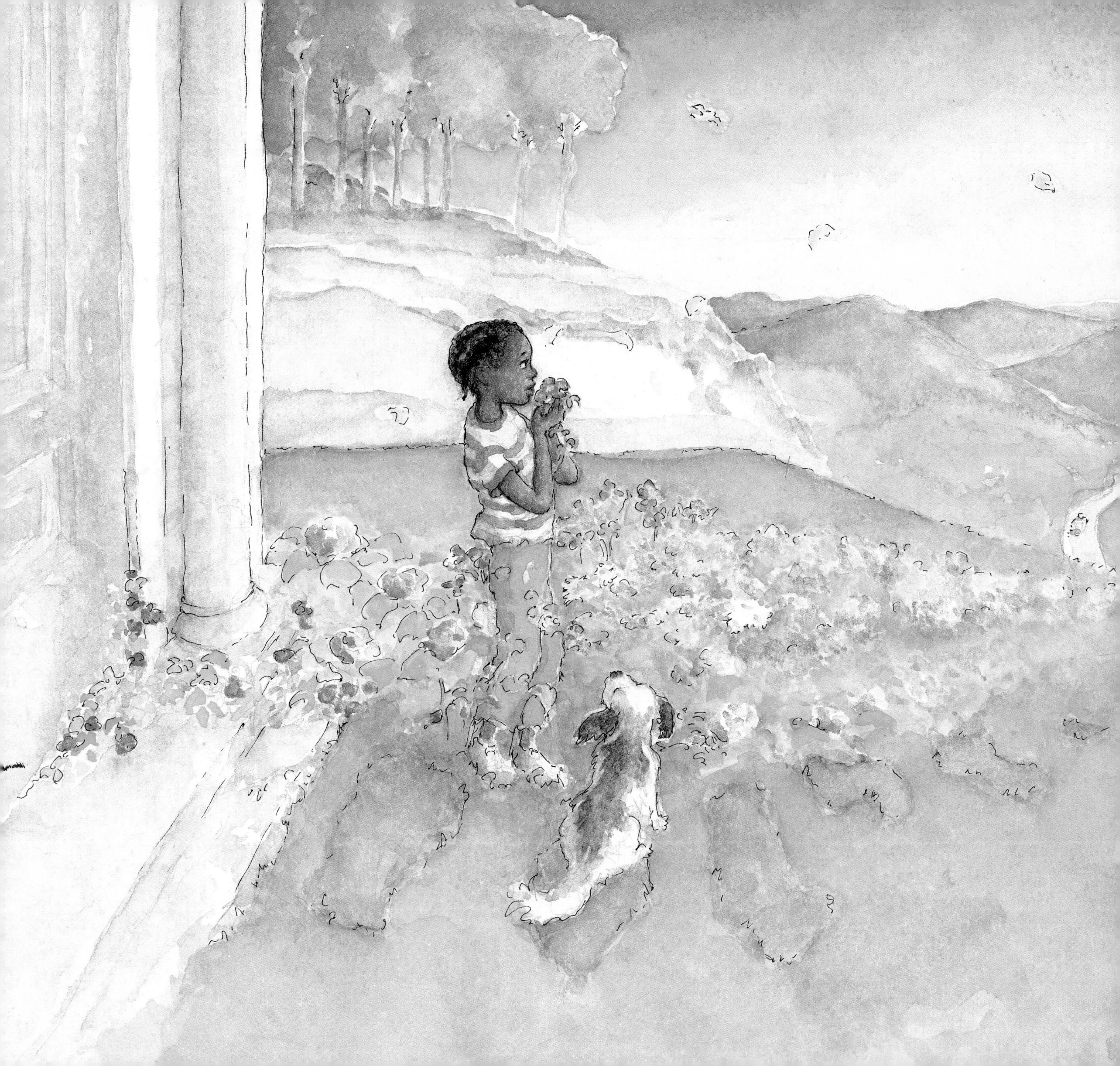

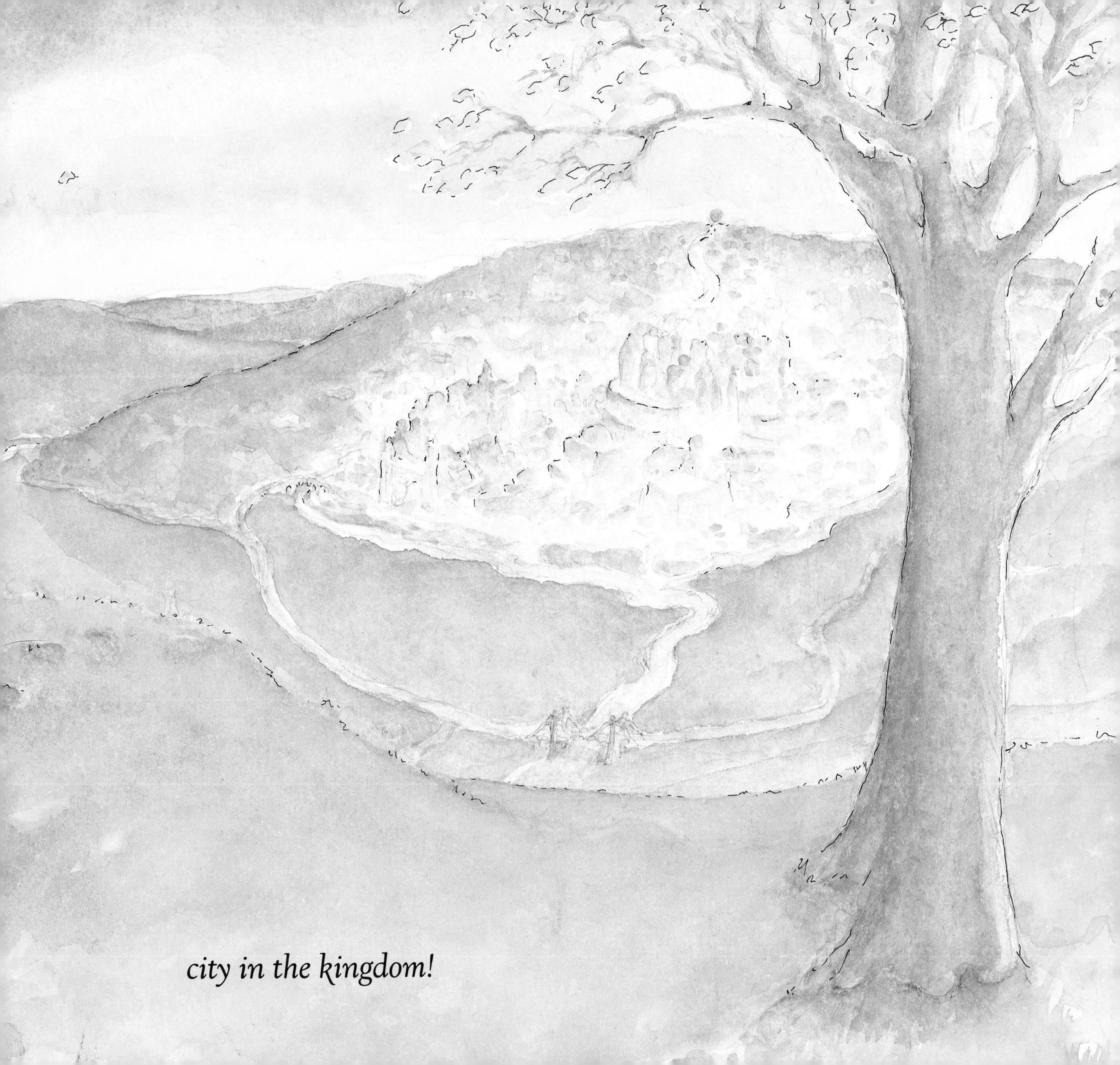

city in the kingdom!

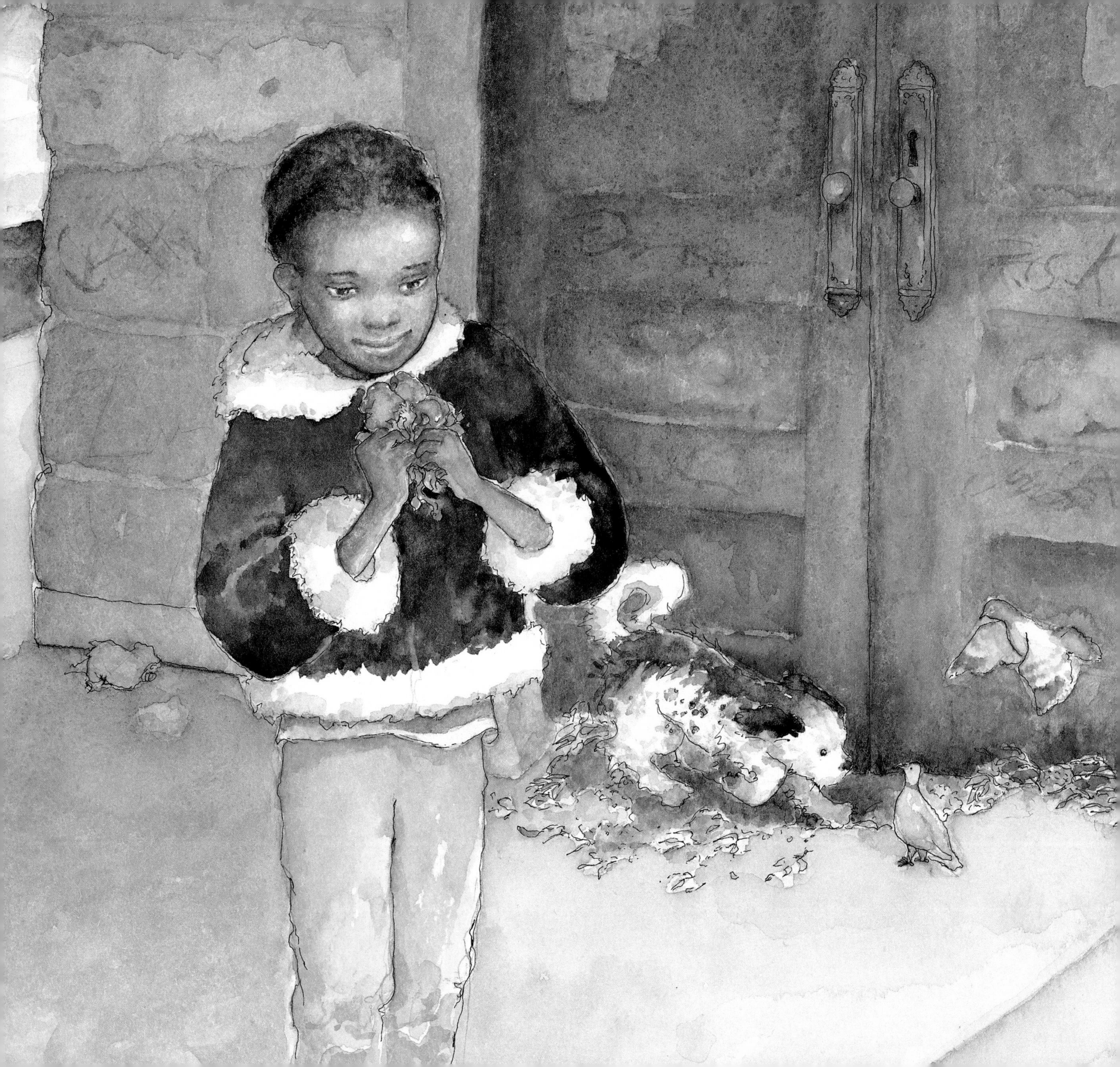

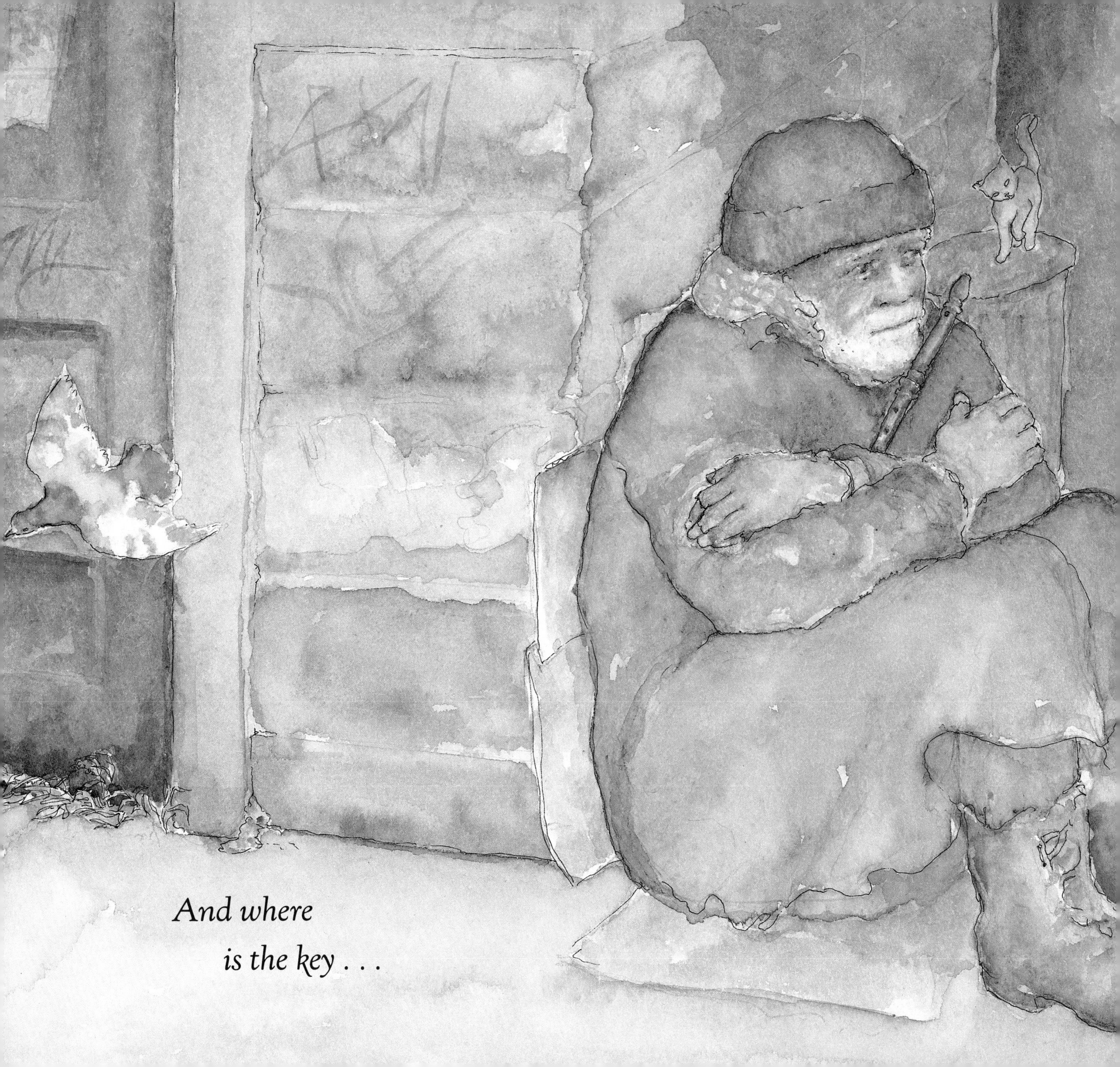

And where
is the key . . .

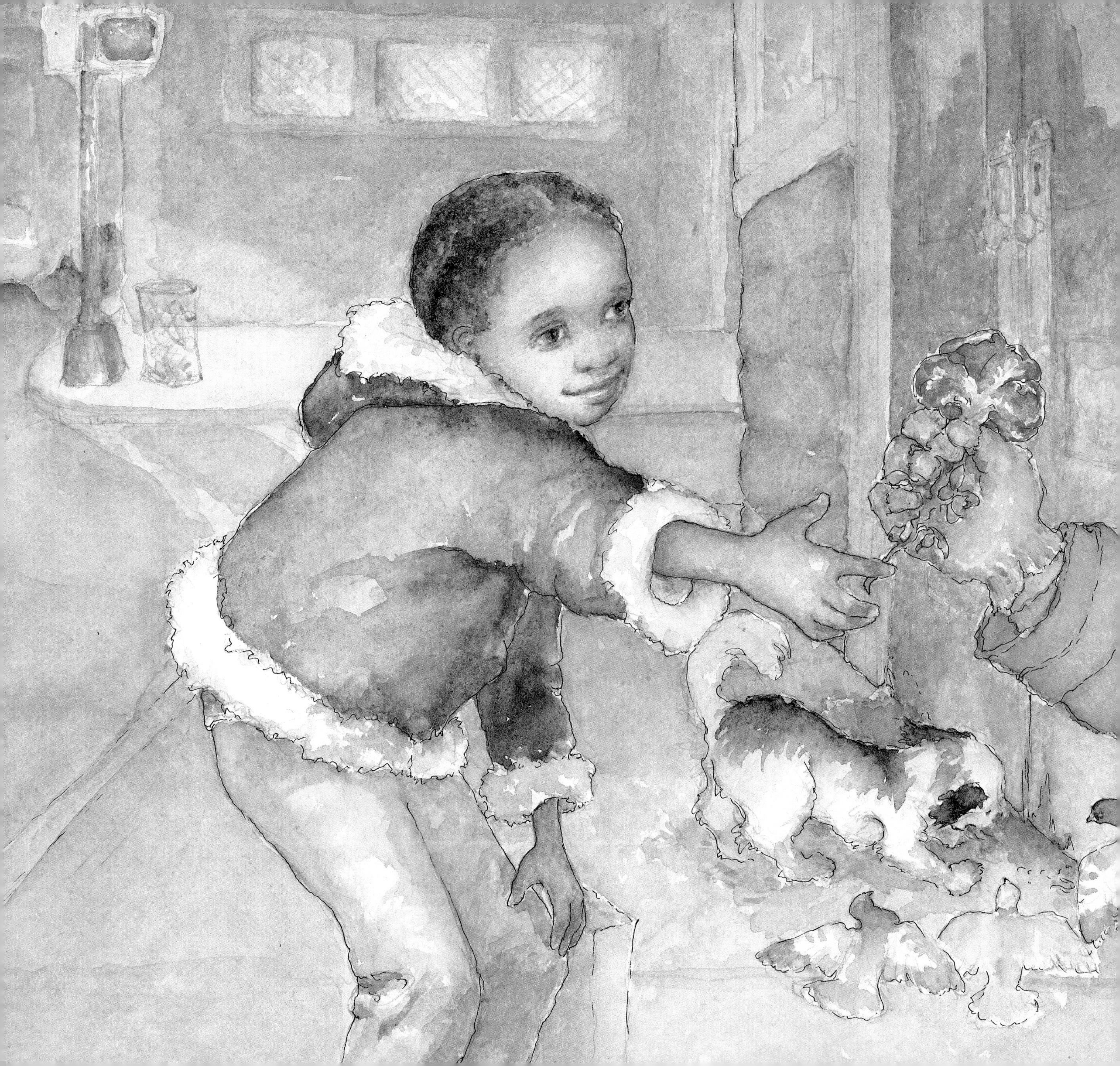

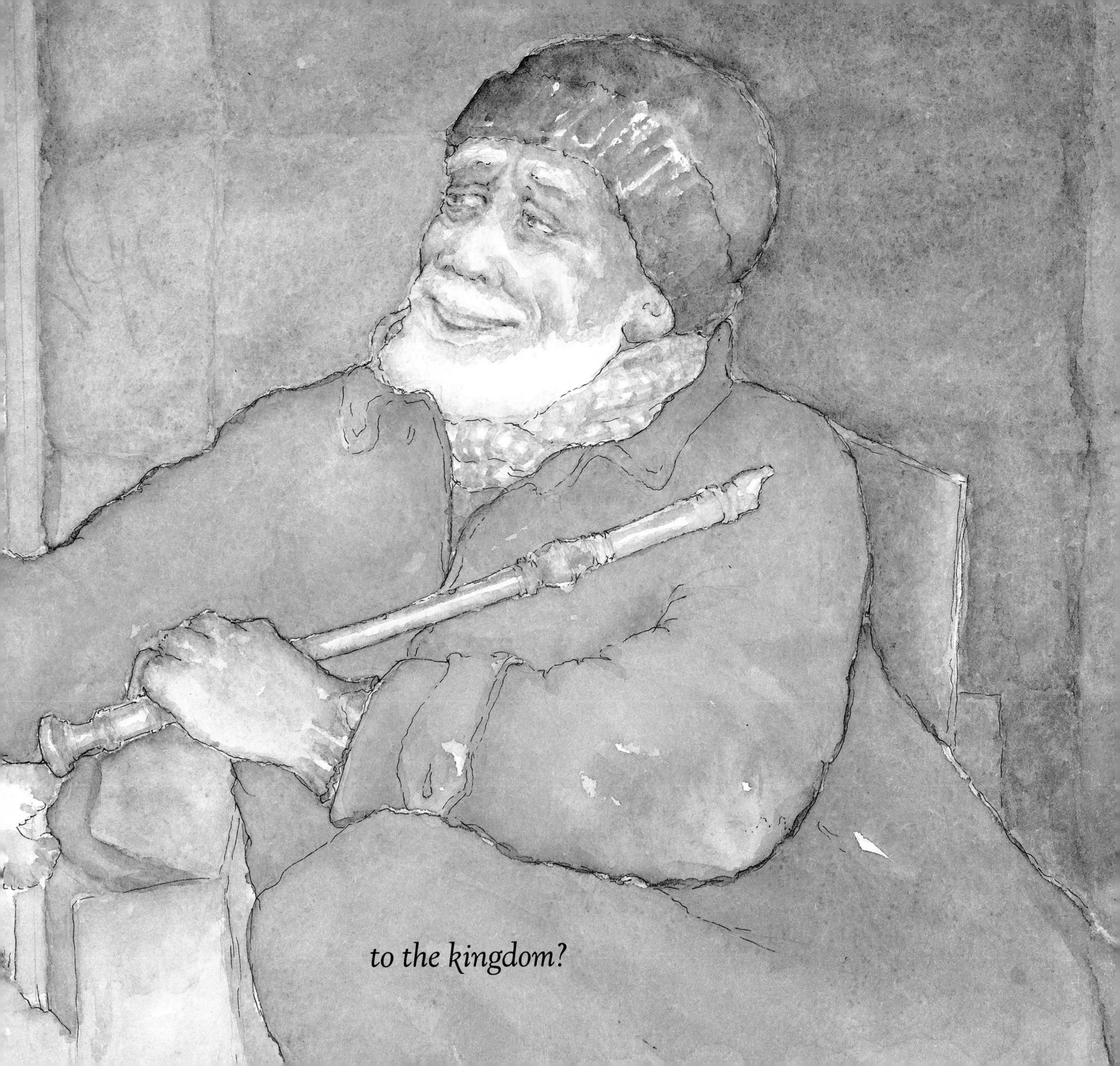

to the kingdom?

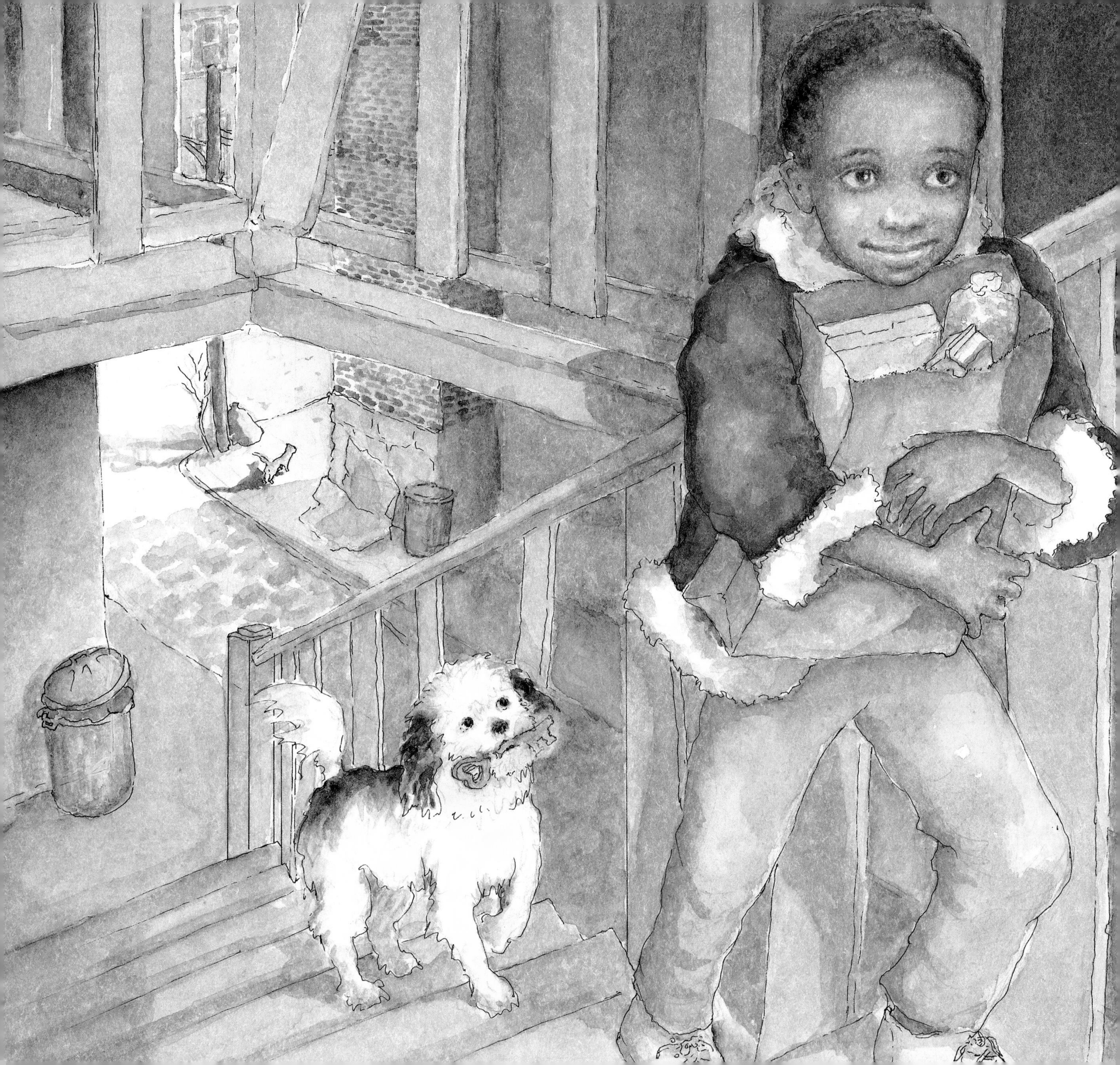